turtle box memories

CHANDRA LYNN SMITH

This book is lovingly dedicated to
the Master Story Teller who stepped into my story
and invited me to create with Him.

"When hard pressed, I cried to the Lord,
he brought me into a spacious place."

Psalm 118:5(NIV)

"He brought me out into a spacious place;
he rescued me because he delighted in me."

2 Samuel 22:20

ACKNOWLEDGMENTS

My deepest gratitude goes to my husband, Don, for believing in me and tolerating the hours I sit at my desk writing and also the many conversations about the lives of the characters in my head. 'ILUVM'

This book would not exist without the shelves of trinkets, rocks, shells, and statues from my four sons, Brandon, Garrett, Eric, and Adam. One day as I sat at my desk I picked up the heart-shaped rock and thought about the day Eric brought it home for me. As I looked at the array of treasures arranged in my office, I thought about the story behind each one. Who'd have thought a heart-shaped rock among other things would inspire a novel? Thank you, my sons.

If I could sit with my sweet Mama, great-Aunt Millie, cousin LouAnn right now I'd thank them for the vacations at Topsail, North Carolina, the inspiration for my fictional island and town of Mimosa Beach.

Thank you George, "Coach", Bugji. Most of the time I do not have any one character modeled after a real person. That is not true Of Kendra's father, Arthur. Coach, every time I wrote a scene about Pa I saw your smile, your eyes, your loving heart, and felt your powerful hugs. Even their serious conversations on the beach when Pa spoke difficult wisdom were taken from similar conversations you and I had when I was in college. Thank you.

Thanks to my beta readers Carolyn, Heavenly, Sue, and Amy. Each of your enthusiasm and heartfelt "I love that story," were great encouragement, especially on the days I almost gave up.

Thank you, thank you, thank you Pat Trainum, Johnnie Alexander, and Renee Osborne, fellow members of Imagine That Writers and writing sojourners with me.

Thanks to my critique partners in the Penwrights Group, Sharpened Pencils, and the ACFW Scribes group. Track changes surely get used a lot and I am grateful for each one. I know I wear your fingers out sometimes. Special thanks to Glenda and Kimberli for taking time out of your busy schedules to read the entire manuscript one more time.

Thanks to my fellow authors of *Coming Home; A Tiny House Collection*. Thank you for inviting me to join you on that project and teaching me about this Indie publishing world. I especially thank Ane Mulligan and Linda Yezak for their untiring answers to my questions.

Thanks to the American Christian Fiction Writers(ACFW) for the wealth of help, information, prayers, and programs available to writers of all genres. Thanks for offering the Genesis Contest for not-yet-published authors.

Thanks to my readers for taking time out of your life to go on a little trip to the beach with me.

CHAPTER ONE

DISCOVERY

Mimosa Beach, North Carolina
Present

endra Michaels kicked off her flip flops and wiggled her toes in the grass. She dropped the clipboard beside the discarded sandals and leaned against the old mimosa tree. That morning she'd pegged and roped three turtle nests. It was the first time she'd ever found them before Memorial Day. Then again, it was the first time in years she'd been here before the holiday.

She lowered herself to Nana's old quilt she'd spread on the ground and rested her head against the tree trunk. A nap would feel wonderful right about now. Her daughters had arrived late last night and they'd all stayed up way too long talking about the future.

Sunlight shining through the leaves made flickering shadows on her outstretched legs. A breeze off the sound brought in the drone of a motor boat. She closed her eyes and absorbed the moment.

Home. Crossing the bridge onto the island a week ago had

been like one long body sigh. So many things different. As many of them the same. But this time she was home to stay.

Opening her eyes and looking into the tree above, she half expected to see Tommy King staring down at her. She shook her head. Many summers and life complications had passed since he hid in those branches.

The screen door banged. Footsteps pounded across the wooden back porch. Kendra sat up as Adrienne and Arielle raced toward her much like they had when they were little girls. But they were college graduates now. Sometimes when she looked at them, she saw the Algebra and Biology teachers, but there were moments, like this one, when she saw two little blonds playing on the beach. Life had skipped by when she wasn't looking.

Adrienne dropped onto the old quit beside Kendra. Her eyes sparkled. "Hurry up, Arielle. Show Mom what we found."

Long-haired, athletic Arielle joined her sister and placed a box on the quilt in front of Kendra. "This was hidden in the back corner of Dad's closet."

Kendra gasped and covered her mouth. She swallowed the lump in her throat. After touching the turtles carved into the lid, she traced the seashell-and-starfish border. Picking it up and gently rocking it made the contents rattle. Dare she hope everything was intact? Memories of a time long past tickled her mind.

Six years ago, when Stanton accused her of cheating, he'd grabbed the box of trinkets and left. Later he told her he'd destroyed it and thrown the pieces away.

Arielle touched her shoulder. "Momma, what is it?"

Adrienne pulled her knees up under her chin and wrapped her arms around her legs. "We didn't open it. Hoped you might share it with us."

Kendra pressed her lips together. What if she told the girls the story associated with each memento? It would mean telling them about Tommy. And Stan's ugly side. She'd spent her marriage protecting their daughters from learning of his infidelities.

Delving into the past would bring that to light and change everything. It would destroy the girl's memories of their father and might even cloud their feelings for her.

"I thought this box was gone. Destroyed. Give me a minute. We'll open it."

She traced the turtle again, then the letters "KLTTLK" below it. Her heart hitched. The touch kindled a memory of Tommy on the night of her first Boardwalk Beach Ball.

Tommy Leon King—eyes as brown as Hershey Kisses, unruly hair bleached by the sun, and a smile that would melt glaciers—pushed the box to her. "I made this for you, Kenna. Thought you could keep all our treasures in it, and when you miss me maybe it will help. And see? Our initials are on the top."

Then he kissed her like he would never stop. But he had stopped. The next year he went away to college. And before Kendra could join him at State the following year everything changed.

She stared at the boat in the sound. After all of these years how could the betrayal and loss still rip the scab off her heart?

"Momma?" Arielle wiped a tear tracking down Kendra's cheek. "If it's going to make you sad, we'll put the box back and forget we found it."

Kendra smiled at them. Sometimes happy and sad dwell in the same memory. She bit her lower lip, closed her eyes and pushed the hurt to a corner of her mind.

"You've always loved my stories. Maybe it's time I tell you a true one. Each item in this box is a story. I will share them, but I don't know how this story ends."

Removing the contents from the box and placing the items on the quilt brought a keen sense of déjà vu. How many hundreds of times had she done this with all of her Tommy treasures? Good memories with bad endings. Her daughters were grown up now. She didn't have to protect them anymore. Besides, Kendra was tired of keeping secrets. Pa always said truth never lied. Stan hated "when the old man says that." No wonder, Stan was all about fabrications. Business trips. Late nights at the office. Promises he'd never do it again.

She gently placed the open box on the quilt beside her treasures. At least breaking the box was a lie she could be glad about.

Arielle interrupted her thoughts.

"You touch that box like it's a priceless treasure."

"It is. I haven't seen it since—well, since the day we buried Pa."

Kendra reached toward one of her treasured mementos then stopped. "Before I go further, umm, I need to tell you your father was not my first love..."

Adrienne nodded. "Well, we've seen enough of your high school photos to know there was only one guy in all of them with you and after high school he was no more. It was easy to figure he was your first love and it went south after you graduated. You never even talked about him. Tell us the story, Mom. We'll get through the tough parts together."

Kendra lined up the gumball-machine rings, heart-shaped rock, and broken sand dollar. But the little pewter turtle, she picked up and slipped into her pocket. It was like finding a long-lost friend. The perfect little conch shell went on top of the note and photo taken at the boat. Memories and hopes kaleidoscoped through her mind. Her heart beat so hard she could feel it in her toes.

She held up the box. "Tommy Leon King gave me this box. He was my first love, my true love." There. She'd said it. "I loved your father, but it wasn't the same. He knew it. He always maintained my heart was unfaithful to him."

Kendra sighed. She wasn't the one who cheated, so why did she feel a tinge of guilt? Of course she had spent years hoping she and Tommy would have a chance one day. She probably hadn't hid it from Stan as well as she thought. But he also should have known she stopped hoping that a long time ago.

"When it comes down to it, in a small way, he spoke the truth."

4

She half-expected them to get up and storm off. Neither moved. Kendra's heart hurt. Her eyes burned. The fact that a box of childhood treasures could turn her to mush meant Tommy had more of a hold on her heart than she'd ever realized or accepted.

Forty-seven was too old to feel like a lovesick teenager. She took a deep breath.

"Tommy graduated a year ahead of me. He worked on his family's farm on the mainland. We planned to go to State together after I graduated. But..." she shrugged. "Your grandmother whisked me off to Europe for six months."

"Why did you agree to go?"

"Looking back, I'm not really sure. Mother and I had been making progress in mending our relationship. She and Pa were working on theirs too. Pa wanted me to go, thought it will help us grow closer. Tommy even thought I should. And promised he'd wait for me. I caved."

More eye burning. Her chest ached.

"He wrote every day at first. Then the letters stopped coming. And he never returned my calls. Mother extended our trip another six months. We went to event after event where she introduced me to the 'important' people. That included the rich and connected Stanton Allen Michaels III."

"But you loved Tommy. Why would you start dating someone else?"

She shook her head. "I didn't. I turned him down each time he asked. But toward the end of the year, Mother handed me a newspaper clipping. It was Tommy King and Samantha Elkins's wedding announcement."

Their eyes widened, and as often happened, voices overlapped. "What?"

"Samantha always chased Tommy. When he never got my replies to his letters, he was distraught and Samantha consoled him. Right into her bed. By the end of my year in Europe, she was pregnant. They quit college to get married and run his family's farm."

"What a jerk." Adrienne twirled a short curl around her index finger. "Even without letters from you, he should've told you before you came home. Did you really never write him?"

"I wrote every single day. Even after he stopped. I mailed them every three days."

Arielle folded her arms across her chest. "It was Grams's fault, wasn't it?"

Kendra stared at her lap. Memories of Pa were the only ones these stories wouldn't tarnish.

"Mom, tell us. It's time." Adrienne said.

"After we got back in the States, I was inconsolable. I ran away to New York, went to business school, and worked as a waitress. I ran into Stanton at a dance club and we started dating. We'd been dating about four months when Mother wrote me a long letter explaining how she wanted more for me than Tommy and local beach life, so after she extended the trip from six months to a year, she intercepted our letters. Years passed before I spoke to her again."

Arielle shook her head. "I don't know how you survived."

Kendra wrung her hands. Because their father was a charmer and she became distracted from her broken heart long enough to believe he was the man for her.

"I was lonely and naïve. Stan swept me off my feet. He offered security. We loved each other, and, for a long time that was enough." She leaned toward them. "He gave me the two most beautiful gifts I could ever ask for."

Arielle's brows knit together. She fiddled with the tiny shell. "Why would Dad hide the box and let you think it was gone?"

Kendra shook her head. She couldn't revisit that night yet. The saddest night of her life. No way was she ready to tackle that one.

"Not yet." She started returning the items to the box. "There are a lot of stories here. We'll take our time going through them. We've got all summer."

Arielle placed the shell in the box. "Momma, what happened to Tommy and Samantha and the baby?"

"She lost their baby in the seventh month. Poor Samantha had two more miscarriages and then never got pregnant again."

"They stayed together?"

"Of course."

"Were they happy?"

She nodded. "Yes. We made peace with each other and sometimes when I came to the island we had dinner together. I saw them several times when she was sick. That was a rough summer for all of us."

"What do you mean?"

"It was tough watching her wither away. This is a small community, and everyone struggled through it."

Hopefully the girls didn't sense there was way more to it than that. It really had been a rough summer, many difficult choices were made. Some of them would surface as she shared everything. The urge to slam the box closed and put it back in the closet overwhelmed. There was joy in the treasures, but lots of pain, too. Wasn't it enough to figure out what life without Stanton looked like?

Adrienne picked up the photo and gawked at it. "Oh my goodness, Mom, your hair and your clothes!"

Kendra chuckled. "Honey, it was the eighties. Big hair, short shorts, cropped tops, and high top sneakers were the rage."

"Well you did rock the look. But, holy cow, that's a lot of hair."

Arielle took the photo and mock gagged. "That's one fashion if it returns I'm not trying." She nudged Adrienne's shoulder. "But I will say this, Tommy was smoking *hot*."

Kendra sighed. "He still is."

CHAPTER TWO

GUMBALL RINGS

Kendra took the photo from Adrienne. A shirtless Tommy stood next to her, smiling. Those eyes still made her heart flutter. She slid her finger across his cheek. The slick paper felt nothing like the three-day scruff he'd sported that day on the boat. It had tickled her fingers.

"The best way to tell a story is from the beginning. We'll get to this photo another time."

Arielle's shoulders drooped. "You always were a stickler for keeping things in order. I don't think I've ever seen you look so happy."

"Stan and I had our happy times. I know I looked that happy when you two were born. Still do when I'm with you."

"Aw, Mom." Adrienne stood up. "How about we go inside and make a picnic before we get started?"

"Sounds good."

After the girls left, Kendra lay back on the quilt.

The feathery mimosa leaves waved and the first pink flowers were just budding. Soon the tree would be in full bloom, and the fragrance would surround her like a soft perfume. She touched the box at her side and thought of her argument with Mother and

Pa about the trip. Why in the world had she let them convince her six months in Europe—that grew into a year's stay— was what she needed after high school? If she'd refused to go and stayed home, maybe Tommy's part in her life would be more than a wood trinket box and memories.

Adrienne's laughter as she exited the house interrupted Kendra's train of thought. Which was probably a good thing. After all, if she had stayed here, she'd have missed the joy her daughters brought to her. Life sure had a way of complicating and confusing.

"Momma, we really do have to grocery shop tomorrow." Arielle placed a tray on the quilt. "This is like a picnic from Old Mother Hubbard's cupboard."

She looked at the stack of sandwiches and bowls of chips and cherries. "Looks like a feast to me." She took a chip and crunched it. "How about Sally's Seafood tonight? I haven't had Crab Imperial like hers since the last time we were here."

Arielle nodded. "Four years ago, right after graduation—" She bit her lip.

Adrienne glared at her.

A curious look passed between them. Kendra remembered that weekend. She had come here alone in the afternoon to get the house ready for the onslaught of friends for a beach weekend. The girls had arrived earlier than expected and in foul moods. They wouldn't talk about it. She'd figured it was a sister spat.

But Stan never came that weekend, and when she asked them why he wasn't with them, they stumbled over some excuse about him not wanting to be around a bunch of rowdy high school grads.

She eyed them. "What am I missing?"

Arielle stared at the quilt. "We can talk about it some other time. Right now, we're having a picnic, and you're sharing your treasures with us."

The girl's stubborn streak was as big as the island was long, and it wouldn't do to push for more information.

Kendra opened the box and retrieved the gumball rings. She slid them on and off her pinky finger. Funny, they'd seemed huge when she was in seventh grade.

"Tommy gave me these on a day I was in the bay pretending to set crab pots. Mostly I was just playing."

🐢

Back yard
Summer after sixth grade

There were a bunch of things I wanted to do. Crabbing in the bay wasn't one of them. But Pa left me a list of chores about a mile long. This was the prettiest day we'd had in months and that Friday everybody would come in for the summer. Tommy and I were supposed to meet at the Rec Park, but I was stuck setting crab traps.

I kicked the water and looked across my backyard toward Tommy's. I'd heard his family arrive late the night before. I hadn't seen him much over the past year. It was like seventh grade and junior high school had abducted my best friend. Guess I wouldn't see him today either. Maybe I wasn't his best friend anymore.

Stupid crabs.

Water splashed behind me and somebody pulled my braid. I spun around ready to smack whoever it was, and Tommy caught my hand mid-swing.

"Hey, Kenna, you gonna play with the crabs all day?"

He still called me 'Kenna.' Still my best friend.

"I'm mostly trying not to. I found a broken sand dollar. Wish I'd find a whole one sometime."

I left my crab cages in the water. Tommy hugged me. "I missed you somethin' awful this year, Kenna. Seventh grade was okay.

11

Junior High was different anyway. Would have been a lot better if the sixth graders were there too. Least then I could have seen you at lunch and snuck up on you sometimes and pulled your braids."

"Didn't miss the braid pullin' one bit, Tommy King," I lied. I crossed my arms and stuck out my tongue at him.

He laughed, grabbed my hand and dragged me to the mimosa tree. I followed him up into the low branches. Then he reached into his pocket and pulled something out, but kept it closed in his fist.

"I got you something. Took about every coin I had in my piggy bank to get the two I wanted. You wouldn't believe all the junk I got out of that gumball machine before I got these."

He opened his palm. There were two silver gumball rings in his hand. One had a white stone, the other gold.

"Your birthstone and mine."

"They're nothin' but fake rings."

"I know that."

"Then why'd you want to spend all your money on them?"

"It's like a promise. You're my best friend ever and one day you're gonna marry me. I just know it. So, I got these rings to make you remember that we have us a destemy."

"Destemy?"

"Or whatever that word is. Like it was all planned out for us?"

I giggled. "You say some of the funniest things. How can you know we're gonna get married? I never even held hands with a boy yet."

"You hold mine all the time."

"That's different. You're not a b—"

"Huh?"

"Aww, shoot, you know what I mean. You're just Tommy."

🐢

Under the Mimosa Tree

Present

"I stuck those rings into my pocket. We spent the afternoon making it look like we were crabbing. Mostly, we just sat in the water's edge and talked. I think I brought two crabs in for supper. But Pa wasn't mad. He almost never got mad at me."

Kendra rolled the rings around in her palm. "I told Tommy I would throw them away the day we finally talked about Samantha. But he asked me not to. Said we never know about the future. I still might need them one day, 'destemy' and all. Then he hugged me and walked out of my life for a long time."

"Tell us about that day."

"Which one?"

"When you talked about Samantha."

Kendra leaned back against the tree trunk. The day that started with a beautiful walk and the promise of happy time spent with her daughters had rapidly diminished into an emotional tidal wave. Wasn't it enough she had to figure out what mourning Stan looked like? Maybe it would have been better if he had destroyed the box, after all. No, that was not true. Somewhere in the sharing would be a blessing.

"After your father and I got married, we bought the house in Richmond. He purchased an office building there. That's when Williams Investments hired TJ Laurence to be your dad's partner. He ran things in New York and the two of them held meetings every few weeks when Stan went up there. Of course, the company jet made commuting an easy task."

Adrienne nodded. "Mom, we know all of that. You're beating around the bush."

"You're right." She stretched her legs out and rested her head on the tree. "I avoided coming home for months. Pa and Mother came to visit us a few times. I hate to say I was not very civil with her. After Christmas she went on one of her trips to the Keys to isolate and write. So, Stan and I went home to visit Pa for New Year's. We had a peaceful time."

She chuckled. "It was probably the first New Year's since Stan became of age that he was sober. He had to fly to the corporate offices January second, so I decided to stay with Pa a few more days before going home."

Kendra took the rings from Adrienne, placed them in the box, and then closed it. She thought of Stan's four-day scruff that morning before he left. How she had loved his natural down-to-earth look better than the businessman. She touched her heart.

"I loved him very much in those days. Whether we were at home, or the beach, or on a weekend away, when he wasn't Mr. Businessman he doted on me. We had so much fun together. That weekend we took several long walks on the beach. I think he liked the winter beach better than summer.

"I'm not delaying. This is part of the story. Pa was doing some police training and the house was just plain empty after Stan left. So I grabbed a chair, a coffee, and walked to the Turtle Shack. Not long after I sat down, I heard some barks and the sandiest, shaggiest Cavalier King Charles Spaniel I'd ever seen raced to me and leaped right into my lap.

"When I turned to look for the human that belonged to the dog, a familiar voice said, 'Kenna, it's you.'"

Turtle Shack
January 1993

"I heard you were in town."

"So, the grapevine is still alive and productive around here?"

"Always. Sorry about the dog attack."

I rubbed salty, wet fur. "She's cute. What's her name?"

"Mimosa."

"Original."

"Yep."

He sat in the sand beside my chair and Mimosa jumped from my lap to his.

"Are you all right?"

I nodded. "I'm married. We live in Richmond. Stan's a good man and I'm happy. How's Samantha?"

"It was a sad Christmas. She had another miscarriage two days after Thanksgiving."

"I heard."

"Kenna, I'm sorry."

I brushed my hair from my face and stared across the inlet. Maybe one day our conversations would again be friendly, but right now, I just didn't know how to speak to him. I did know that God would want me to accept his apology.

"I forgive you. And, I'm sorry you lost another baby. Maybe next time."

"Maybe."

He stood back up and walked a few feet toward the surf.

"I really messed up Kenn—"

"Call me Kendra. I think it's only appropriate—all things considered."

His shoulders slumped. "You're right."

"You know, I'm so silly, I still have those two gumballs rings. I should probably just throw them away."

"You throw a trinket away? Never."

He faced me and gave me his crooked grin. "Just keep them. Memories and that stuff. Besides, you never know what the future holds... 'destemy' and all."

🐢

Under the Mimosa Tree
Present

Arielle picked up the photo Kendra hadn't put in the box. "I love that he wanted you to keep them, and you did. Will you tell us about the picture now?"

Kendra shook her head. "I need to take a walk. I want to make sure those nests I found this morning have not been disturbed. Will you two clean up our picnic and take the box back inside? Just leave it on the coffee table. I'll be back in time for supper."

"Sure, Mom. We can go through more of Dad's things. For someone who didn't spend much time at the beach, he sure left a bunch of stuff here."

"Your father did a lot of strange things."

"True that." Adrienne threw her arm over Arielle's shoulder as they headed to the house.

Kendra walked to the other side of the island. She reached inside her pocket and felt the turtle. She smiled. "We'll talk about turtles at supper."

CHAPTER THREE

PEWTER TURTLE

On the Beach
Present

*K*endra marked the third nest then strolled up the beach. At low tide the walk to water's edge was half a football field. Funny, when she was a child, that was the distance at high tide. It used to take forever to get to the water at low tide. Erosion sure changed the beachscape.

She stuck her toe in a receding wave. Emotional erosion changed heart-scapes too. Sometimes she questioned if she even knew her heart anymore. How could she still harbor deep emotions for Tommy after all this time? Had she lied to herself for years that she had nothing but friendship for him? Stan must have known the truth, or at least sensed it.

Kendra spoke to the waves or sky or nothing in particular. "That's no excuse. Why am I trying to excuse his unfaithfulness? When he cheated on me two weeks after our first anniversary he knew I was committed to him. Every time he came back to me all remorseful I always forgave and took him back. Then he'd go have another and try to cover it up. I'm not sure he worried that much about what I did or how I felt. Sure my heart hurt, but I was faithful. He thought he could ease his conscience by telling me I was the only one he loved. I'll not lay his guilt at my feet."

At the edge of the rock jetty Kendra stopped and sat. She stared across the blue expanse. An all-too-familiar scent drifted from beside her.

Tommy.

"I heard you were back in town."

She exhaled and smiled. Of course he would find her.

"Hey."

"Mind if I pull up some jetty?"

"Help yourself."

He sat beside her, stretched his long legs in front of him and stared ahead. The comfortable silence between them enveloped her with peace.

"Welcome home, Kenna. Sorry about Stan."

She hugged her knees and rested her cheek on them, facing him. How could he still be the most handsome man she'd ever known?

He picked up a rock and pitched it beyond the waves.

"Are you here to stay this time?"

Kendra tossed one also. It dropped into the ocean close to his. "Once the estate is settled and I sell the house, I'll be here."

"Still managing your boarding kennels?"

"No. I am kind of in between things right now. I sold all four of them a few years ago. I just didn't have the heart to run them without Pa's partnership. I'll manage the turtle patrols this summer and then decide what's next after Adrienne and Arielle move to Wilmington."

"You were quite the entrepreneur."

"I loved being one for a long time. Now I just want to stop."

"And what kind of dogs do you have?"

"None."

His jaw dropped and eyebrows wrinkled. "Your house without a dog or ten? How can that be?"

"Last winter Jasper died. Stan made my life miserable every time I mentioned getting another one. I don't like to housebreak in winter anyway, so I decided to wait until summer. Then the accident happened, and here I am."

He touched her shoulder. "It's summer now."

"That it is. I'll get one once we're settled in."

How she wished she could lean into him, ditch the small talk, and share everything that weighed on her mind.

A wave crashed against the rocks and drenched them. The cool water, the salt on her face, and him beside her was almost too natural. She shouldn't get comfortable with this. She wiped her face with her T-shirt sleeve then stood.

"I'd better head home. The girls and I are going to Sally's for *crab Imperial*. It was good to see you again, Tommy." She meant that even though it sounded like a dismissal.

He rose and offered his hand as they stepped off of the jetty.

"I'm sure I'll see you around. You might suggest your daughters come to my waterpark. A lot of twenty-somethings come in on the weekends."

"That would be good for them." She chuckled. "It will get old hanging out with Mom all the time."

They stood on the beach facing each other. For a minute she thought he would kiss her. And she knew she wanted him to even though she knew there were too many years of estrangement between them for that to happen.

Tommy held her hand to his mouth and placed a soft kiss on the top of her wrist.

"Bye for now, Kenna."

Sally's Seafood Restaurant

Present

The waitress cleared the plates then brought coffee. Kendra watched Arielle sip her caramel mocha and get an instant whipped cream mustache. She smirked above the rim of her mug.

Adrienne rolled her eyes. "Didn't Grams ever teach you how much more refined black coffee is?"

"Yep." Arielle scowled. "But it tastes horrid. I'll stick with the sweet stuff."

The look on her daughter's face matched the one she'd always used when Mother made her try some new gourmet food. Mother's efforts to make Kendra fit into high society failed miserably. Pa always said you couldn't make a turtle change its shell until it was ready. Kendra was never ready.

She removed the turtle from her pocket and placed it on the table in front of them.

"I carried this turtle in either my pocket or my wallet from the summer of 1981 until your father and I got married. It's been in the box ever since."

She picked up her glass and swirled the water. Sometimes memories swept in and warmed the soul. But others whooshed in, wiped out the calm and ushered in a torrent of sadness. She braced herself for the torrent.

"Mother left that summer. Back in those days, I called her Ma. Years later, when she flitted back into my life, she became Mother."

"Now I get it." Adrienne waved her index finger. "No wonder you wanted to be Momma or Mom and never Mother. That was not a term of endearment to you."

Kendra nodded.

"She just left, didn't even say goodbye. Gave me a good-night kiss when I went to bed, and was gone when I got up.

"It was July Fourth. I got up that day all excited about the festival. The regatta ran in the sound all day long. We would sit on our porch, in the yard, or on the pier and watch everything. The day ended with a fireworks display that was like watching colored rain over the water.

"I ran downstairs and grabbed a banana on my way outside. Pa stopped me and swooped me into his big hug. I hadn't ever seen such sadness in his eyes."

Kendra swallowed. Sharing happy moments was fine. But talking about the heartbreaks was like grabbing a scar and ripping it wide open again.

"He sat me down on the porch steps and told me Mother was gone. Said she was like a hummingbird that had to fly away for a while. Told me she would come back one day, but he didn't know when.

"He held me tight and told me he would never leave me. Said he'd make sure I always knew how much he loved me." .

She picked up the turtle and gently enveloped it in her hand.

"Pa started getting me up before the sun each morning to go on turtle walks. It was our time. We walked the beaches, sometimes just us and sometimes with a few other people. We'd find the sea turtle nests and put little fences around them. Then we'd attach a chart to the fence with the date so we'd know when they would hatch.

"Tommy often came with us. In the wee morning hours one day, we found a big leatherback turtle just as she finished covering her nest. She shed these huge tears. Pa said they were normal. I didn't believe him.

"I followed that turtle to the breaking waves and told her she didn't have to leave her babies—that she could stay with them, and I would protect her. I climbed onto her back and rode her to the water."

Kendra opened her palm again and looked at the turtle.

"Pa followed me into the waves. I think I would have ridden that turtle straight into the ocean. I didn't care. When he lifted me off the turtle's back, I collapsed in his arms, crying. He carried me home. Tommy tagged along, and when we got home, I heard Pa tell him I'd be all right. But I knew I wouldn't. Pa was wrong about something else. Ma wasn't like the hummingbird that would come back some day. She was the turtle that left her child behind.

"He tried to tuck me back in bed, but I couldn't sleep. I grabbed my quilt and went out to the tree. Tommy was waiting for me."

🐢

The MimosaTtree
July 5, 1982

"Hey, Kenna, you okay?"
   "No."
"Wanna talk?"
   "No."
"Okay then." He whistled. Real annoying-like.
"Stop that."
"What?"
"Whistlin'."
"Well, aren't you just a joy to be around." He sat cross-legged in front of me. "I got something for ya, but ain't gonna give it to ya if you stay in your turtle shell."

I glared at him. "Not in a turtle shell."

"Sure ya are. Whenever something' upsets you, you're just like a turtle. Ya scrunch up all inside yourself and won't let no one in —not even me."

He nudged me. "Come on, Kenna; your ma ran away, not me."

All my fight left. He was right. He and Pa were all I had left. I better not shut him out. I leaned against him. He wrapped me in his arms and held me tight. It wasn't like the hugs we always gave each other. It was like we connected in a different kind of way. My heart thumped, and my palms got all sweaty.

And I liked it.

Tommy kissed the top of my head and then reached in his pocket and pulled out something tiny. "I got this the other day so you'd have something to remind you of our turtle walks this summer. Figured you could keep it wherever you have the rings."

"What makes you think I still have them?"

"I know you."

"They're in a handkerchief in my drawer. I ain't found the proper place for them yet." I pointed to his closed hand. "So what's that?"

He opened his palm and placed a tiny pewter turtle in my hand. "It's little and cute like you."

I closed it into my hand and held it to my chest.

Tommy wiped my cheek. "Aw now, Kenna, don't cry again. This was s'posed to make you smile. How about you only remember the good parts of this summer?"

"Don't think there are any."

"'Course there are." He gave me his crooked grin and puffed his chest. "Everything about me is a good part."

Tommy sure knew how to make me smile.

"Kenna, look up." He tilted my chin so I could look in his eyes. Then he gave me my first-ever kiss. It was sloppy. And sweet. And I wanted a hundred more. And I couldn't talk.

Guessed he couldn't either, cuz he clamped his mouth shut and pulled away from me. Pretty sure if it was daytime I'd a seen his face turn as red as his ma's strawberries.

I put the turtle in my pocket, jumped up and raced toward the pier, yelling, "Last one in's a rotten egg."

Sally's Seafood Restaurant

Present

Kendra turned to the girls. "I beat him by a leap as we both jumped off the pier in our cutoffs and T-shirts. And I made sure that turtle stayed in my pocket."

"A night swim and Papa didn't mind?"

"Pa was sitting on the back porch watching. He never let me go outside like that at night without being close by. When Tommy left and I went to the house, Pa held a towel for me and wrapped me up in it."

Arielle finished her coffee, leaned back in her chair and nodded. "That was a great story, Momma. I can't wait to meet this Tommy character. He still lives on the island, right?"

"Yes." Kendra rolled the turtle in her palm. "I saw him today."

Adrienne spewed her coffee. "You what? And you didn't tell us?"

"I'm telling you now." Kendra downed her latte and peered at them over the rim of the mug. "It's been a long day. Let's go home."

"Mom, you can't do that to us. It's like when we were little and you offered us morsels instead of whole brownies." Adrienne crossed her arms and set her chin in defiance. "I'm not leaving until you tell us."

"I was on the beach, and there he was. He told me he was sorry about Stan. We sat on the there a while, then I came home, and he went wherever he went." She touched the top of her wrist where he planted the kiss. She'd keep that information to herself. Time for a subject change.

"I thought I heard you talk about going out tonight?"

They nodded. "We're meeting the summer gang for dancing. We'll take you home and then head back out."

"That's not necessary. Take my Jeep, I can walk from here. It will do me good. See you tomorrow."

Kendra stepped into the cool evening air and inhaled deeply.

Salt and sand and French Fries. Ah. The day's memory flood had been almost too much. Then seeing Tommy derailed her.

Kendra got halfway across the yard but stopped at the sound of canine whimpers coming from the front of the house. They got louder, then turned into howls. Some poor puppy was suffering.

"Lord, don't let it have been hit by a car."

She raced to the front and steeled her heart for the worst. The road was clear except for one lone man walking away from her driveway. She'd know that gait anywhere.

She started to follow him, but more howls drew her. They came from a huge cardboard box sitting on the porch just outside the door. She hurried to it, and an adorable Cavalier King Charles Spaniel puppy looked up at her. An envelope was taped to the side of the box.

She picked up the puppy and took him into the yard, then sat on the grass. He circled around her, then climbed into her lap and licked her hand holding the envelope. The single word on the outside of the envelope made her hands tremble.

"Kenna."

She removed a small notecard.

Kenna,

It has come to my attention this house that always had Cavaliers ruling the roost is without one. How sad for those wood floors not to get new scratch marks on them! I was shocked to find out you are dog-free, especially at this difficult time in your life.
This little guy is one of my sweet Emma's pups. She had five, and I sold the others. This guy was too sweet to sell. I named him after the man I respected most in this life. I call him "Arthur."

25

She dropped the letter in her lap. Tommy named the puppy after Pa? Stan had never said one good word about her father, had always called him the old man at the sea.

She held the puppy to her chest. He plastered her with kisses as she inhaled puppy breath.

"Hey, Arthur." He cocked his head and looked into her eyes. "Do you already know your name?"

She picked up the note and finished reading.

Please accept Arthur as my housewarming gift. Plus, it's Mother's Day on Sunday. But if you cannot keep him, I will understand and take him back. I hope there is room in your life for him. He's ten weeks old and has his first shots. I'll have Doc Mason send the vaccination records.

I look forward to seeing him on the beach with you.

Always,
Tommy

How could she keep the pup?

How could she not?

The little guy curled into a ball in her lap and closed his eyes. He knew he was home.

CHAPTER FOUR

THE TURTLE BOX

Home
Present, Mother's Day

*A*s Kendra replaced the lid on the aloe gel a little chill chased across her bare shoulders. She grabbed the old afghan from the back of the sofa and wrapped up in it. Tomorrow she should spend more time in the shade.

Arielle entered the room with an armful of candles of various sizes. After arranging them on the coffee table and the mantel, she picked up the aloe, touched Kendra's shoulders and chuckled.

"Momma, the sunscreen cabinet by the door is still well stocked, right?"

"Always."

"Um-hm. I was just wondering." She grabbed the lighter from the desk drawer and began lighting the candles. A bright flash of lightning lit the night sky, and the lights flickered. "I thought I was doing this for mood, but maybe it's a good thing."

Arielle leaned into the kitchen. "Is that hot chocolate almost ready, sis? We may not have power much longer."

Kendra couldn't make out Adrienne's response, but most likely it was a comment about not rushing perfection. The same one Pa had always made when they impatiently awaited his chocolate delight.

The puppy slept on the rug at her feet. After church they spent the day walking on the beach, swimming in the bay, and having a cookout on the pier. He was worn out. Had he really only been with them since Friday? He'd moved into her heart so fast she felt like he'd been there for weeks.

Her mouth watered when she heard Adrienne spray whipped cream into their mugs. The aroma of rich chocolate preceded Arielle as she entered, carrying a tray loaded with yummy goodness.

As Arielle placed mugs of cocoa and a basket of biscotti on the coffee table, Adrienne retrieved the turtle box from the desk and set it on Kendra's lap.

She traced the turtle as she'd done hundreds of times over the years. If only she could think of a way to talk about the box itself and leave out the reason their father had it. But she had promised the truth.

Arielle set a large vanilla-scented pillar candle on the coffee table.

Kendra took a sip and licked the cream mustache from her lips.

"Adrienne, you outdid yourself this time. Did you add caramel too?"

She nodded.

After dipping her biscotti in the hot beverage and crunching on it, Kendra placed the box on the coffee table beside Adrienne's tray.

"In the order of things, the box is actually next."

Arielle frowned. "Momma, why'd Dad have the box, and why did you think it was gone?"

She opened her mouth, but her words stuck somewhere in her throat. No one knew about the ultimatum Stan had issued that night or the tough decisions she'd made.

"I don't want to talk about that today. I'll not speak ill of him tonight."

Adrienne squeezed Kendra's hands, then nodded at her sister. Arielle sighed.

"Then we will. We knew he was a scoundrel."

A kettle drum beat in Kendra's chest. "I never wanted you to know. In his weird way he did love me. And he adored you two. You have to know that."

Adrienne grumbled something and twirled her hair around her finger. "Mom, the weekend after graduation when we got here earlier than you expected, it was because we had to get away. We came home from Stacy's celebration, and Dad was in the pool. With someone. Not swimming."

Arielle made a gagging noise. "I never swam in our pool again."

Kendra gasped. He had the nerve to bring his other woman home and was bold enough to be outside? Her hands closed into fists and she gritted her teeth so hard her jaw hurt.

Arielle set her mug down. "That was four years ago. We dealt with it in our own way. But that's why we hardly spoke to him or spent time with him that summer whenever he came to the beach. I loved Dad, but it was never the same after that. I always felt guilty for not telling you. I thought you didn't know."

"Yeah, I guess we thought we had to protect you." Adrienne bit her lower lip. "Codependency at its finest."

Kendra twisted her hair into a bun. So each of them thought they protected the other. Goodness, it really was time to end all of the secrets.

"I knew from the very first time he had an affair. I never had one and he knew that. But he also knew my heart was divided. How he got the box is actually part of the sand dollar story. Tonight, we'll just talk about when Tommy gave it to me."

She held it out to them. "He made it. The summer before I started tenth grade, we became a couple. Or rather, we acknowledged our couple status. Neither of us had gone with anyone else all through junior high, but we told everyone we were just friends. Things changed that summer."

Home
June 1987

I stood in front of my dresser, tears streaming down my cheeks. I needed my mom at a time like this, and she was too busy promoting her latest novel-turned-movie to come and spend even one summer week with me. If she showed up tonight, I wouldn't talk to her anyway.

Sitting on my vanity stool in front of the mirror, I wished I had gotten that Dorothy Hamill cut like everyone else so I wouldn't have to mess with my hair. I threw my hairbrush across the room and my bed where the dune of dresses was piled. What was I going to wear? Not one was deemed worthy of the Board-walk Beach Ball.

The city hall clock chimed five times. Oh great. Tommy would be here in a half hour. My hair wasn't done, I didn't have a dress to wear, and my mascara was smeared from my stupid tears.

I put my head on my arms on my vanity and screamed.

The front door opened and closed. Pa's feet pounded up the stairs. He stopped outside my door and knocked.

"I found it, Kendra. You decent? Can I come in?"

I quickly slipped into my robe then opened the door. I must have looked horrible because he tossed the garment bag on my bed and enveloped me in his big hug.

"What's wrong with my girl? I thought you were excited about tonight." He touched my cheek and wiped a smudge under my eye. "And look at you. You're about broken, I think."

Broken? Leave it to Pa to find the right word.

"I can't get my hair up, my makeup is running, and I don't have a new dress like all the other girls. If I had a mother who cared I wouldn't have to humiliate myself going to a dance looking like a freak."

I glared at my reflection. "Tommy won't ever ask me on another date after he sees me."

Pa pulled the bobby pins out of my hair, then reached for the garment bag he'd tossed aside.

"I think I can help you with your hair. We both know I am the only police chief in North Carolina who can do amazing braided updos. Probably one of only a few men who knows what an updo is. While you do not have a new dress, you have an old one. One your mother wore to our first Boardwalk Beach Ball."

Unzipping the bag, he revealed a tea-length, turquoise satin dress with spaghetti straps. I might have to melt and be poured into it. Wasn't sure I had enough curves to pull it off. But my goodness, if I could, I'd have the loveliest dress at the dance!

He hung the dress on the door and turned me toward the dresser. "You sit down right there, and I'll fix this mess you made of your hair. The makeup thing is up to you, though."

I loved when Pa braided my hair. Ever since Ma left, he treated me like it was the greatest honor in the world for him to do it. And, true to his word, in no time Pa had braided my hair and twisted it into a bun that almost looked like a tiara.

He kissed the top of my head. "Fix that makeup and try that dress on. I'll be waiting downstairs."

After washing my face and redoing the makeup, I began to feel a little more human. I stared at the dress. Now or never.

It was a perfect fit. I had enough curves, after all. Tomorrow I would be climbing trees and hunting turtles again, but tonight... well, tonight I could be a princess.

Pa and Tommy waited for me at the bottom of the stairs. I'm not sure which one gasped the loudest. When I saw Tommy all dressed up in that brown suit and holding a wood box I about tripped over my own feet. He was the handsomest boy ever.

He handed me the box. "I made this for you from the old cypress tree in our yard. We had to cut it down after the storms last summer. Thought you might like to keep your treasures in it."

I didn't know what to say. It was beautiful. I traced the carvings on the lid and then opened it. Nestled in a bed of tissue was a corsage made of roses, and of all things, mimosa blossoms. It smelled prettier than anything. Ever. Well maybe except for Tommy's aftershave.

I handed it to him and faced him so he could put it on me. Oh yeah, his aftershave won the prize. He was nervous about pinning the corsage on my dress. His hands shook so bad I thought for sure he would stab me in the chest.

As he pinned it on me, I stood on tiptoes and kissed his cheek. His face turned as pink as the flowers.

🐢

Home
Present

Kendra remembered that night as if it had just happened. She'd been a princess for a few hours. It was one of the best times of her life.

Placing the box on the coffee table, she kissed her index finger and touched the turtle carving.

"I took the box to the dance that night. Tommy made me leave it in the car. But afterward, when we were parked at the end of the island, watching the moon and the waves and kissing a bunch, I asked him about the initials.

"He kissed his index finger and touched it to the turtle, then, did the same with mine. "It stands for Kendra Loves Tommy and Tommy Loves Kendra."

She took the box to the credenza and set it beside the crystal vase Pa had given her. Two very different things, but each a priceless treasure.

Arthur chose that moment to wake and race around the house from front door to back. Was he a puppy or a whirling dervish?

"Time for him to go out. Maybe he can take care of his business between raindrops and lightning flashes."

Adrienne followed her outside and trudged around the yard. She nudged her.

"You know, Mom, just like we have sunscreen in the cupboard, we have an umbrella right by the back door."

"Never have liked them."

"I gotta ask you something."

"Yes?"

"Has it occurred to you that Tommy may still be in love with you too?"

Kendra froze and stared at her daughter. Was she that transparent? "Who says I'm in love with him? I was married to your father for twenty-seven years. It's been longer than that since Tommy was in my life."

"We see your eyes when you speak of him. That's love. You were here less than a week when he found you on the beach. That same day he gave you a puppy he named after your father. He still loves you."

Kendra shook her head. This was too much. She turned toward the house and dragged Arthur in. "Come on, puppy; it's time to go to bed."

Adrienne giggled. "Truth is hard to take sometimes, isn't it? Just know, we love you, and we want happiness for you. Sure seems to us like Tommy might be the one to bring that."

"I take it you've talked about this?"

"Of course."

Long after they went inside, Kendra stood at the back door staring at the storm-crested water.

CHAPTER FIVE

HEART-SHAPED ROCK

Home
Present

Kendra stepped onto her front porch and inhaled the salty air. Memorial Day weekend officially ushered in the opening of the summer season. The steady flow of traffic onto the island began Wednesday, but would grow exponentially throughout today. She used to sit on her porch all day long waiting for the Kings to pull into their drive across the street.

She stared at the vacant lot and shoved the emptiness in her heart back into its corner. Hurricane Irene had been selective in which houses she destroyed. The Kings' was one of those lost. The last time she'd seen the house intact, they'd been sitting on her porch before Pa's funeral. Tommy had told her about Samantha's cancer. He said when she got sick they'd stayed at the beach most of the time, but it never felt like he belonged there after she died. So he sold it and bought an oceanfront bungalow.

That night, as he talked about Samantha's sickness and caring for her Kendra realized Tommy really had loved his wife. She'd forgiven the two of them long ago, and it pleased her to know he had been happy.

Because, despite his issues, she'd loved Stan and he'd loved her —as best he could. They really did have happy times in between the difficult ones. He dearly loved his daughters and certainly provided for all of them.

Between both of their financial assets she'd get the house renovated, winterized and up to hurricane code. She wouldn't have to work unless she chose to. She'd heard the owner of Coffee Therapy Café was looking to sell. That might be a fun endeavor. Or not. At least thanks to Mother and Pa's investments, and Stan's inheritance there was no rush to make a decision.

Kendra put Arthur's leash on him and jogged to the beach. It was time to mark the new turtle nest. With the puppy leash in one hand and carrying the bucket with shovel, orange netting, clipboard, and markers in the other, she must look a sight. Every island had its one eccentric resident. If the tourists saw her like this, they'd think it was her.

At the nest, she tethered Arthur to one of her pegs. Couldn't have the turtle lady's dog upset a nest. After staking a perimeter around the nest, she attached the orange netting to the posts. She nailed a No Trespassing sign on each post, wrote the date she found the nest on one of the stakes, and posted the same information on her clipboard. The loggerheads would hatch in forty-five to fifty-five days. She and the rest of the turtle crew would be on the beach each night with spotlights in case they hatched at night. The lights would show the tiny turtles the way to the ocean.

After a long peaceful walk around Mimosa Beach and the sound Kendra turned in toward home. In the back yard she picked some mimosa blossoms and cut a few of the roses from Pa's bushes. Arranging them in the blue crystal vase and placing them on the table beside the heart-shaped rock made her smile. The girls were going to love this story.

They'd been in Wilmington all day looking at houses. Hopefully they were successful. It would make the summer more enjoyable if they weren't fretting over where they'd live when their first teaching jobs started in August.

Kendra showered and dressed in short order. She poured some tea and sat at her desk. Might as well tackle the mail and bills she'd been ignoring all week. She'd hear them get home. Those brand new sports cars were not quiet. Stan had insisted they needed them for college graduation. Adrienne's was red, and Arielle's chameleon. He had paid a small fortune to get them custom painted, but then nothing was too good or expensive for his daughters.

How easily she distracted herself from the mail. Grr. Thumbing through the envelopes her one large stack became three little ones; junk, sympathy cards, and bills. The last letter, from Stan's attorney had pretty much been mocking her since it arrived a week ago.

Kendra put on her reading glasses and grabbed the letter opener. Delaying didn't make it go away. Besides, maybe it was a letter about finalizing the estate so she could close that chapter of her life for good.

Leaning back in the chair she scanned the mail.

Words like investigation...intentional...pending reports... sheriff's department...might as well have been punches to her chest. She sank into the chair. Stan's accident wasn't a result of his careless speeding. Someone wanted him dead? Who in the world could hate him that much?

The back door opened, startling her. How had she not heard the cars? Kendra shoved the letter in the envelope and stuck it under the stack of bills. "Lord, help me be normal. You know I can't deal with that letter right now."

Adrienne and Arielle walked in carrying groceries. As they unloaded them onto the counters, they both spoke at once.

"We brought goodies."

Arielle faced Kendra. "Wilmington is bigger than I remembered. But we found two perfect places. Mine's a cute rancher in a quiet neighborhood. Adrienne opted for a townhouse near the high school. The real estate agent is doing the paperwork. You have to come see them."

"It's so exciting." Adrienne was at the stove opening take-out cartons.

Arielle crossed the room and picked up the rock Kendra had set on the table. She grinned. "Is this the next story?"

Kendra nodded.

"Great! We brought Brunswick Stew and hush puppies. You can tell us all about it while we eat."

"Maybe I want you to tell me about your houses."

"Oh, we will. But we talked about the next story all the way home. You have to go first."

Adrienne placed the carryout on the table, and then grabbed the tea pitcher, napkins and silverware. In no time they were sitting at the formal dining room table, enjoying their feast in paper bowls.

Kendra picked up the rock and rolled it in her hand.

"Mother came home the summer after tenth grade, a few weeks after the Beach Ball. I hadn't seen her since I was ten years old. There had been short letters off and on. They were always about what she had written or published, or where she was traveling for movies made from her books or screen plays. She never asked how Pa was, or me.

"So, when she showed up out of the blue that June, I wasn't happy to see her."

🐢

Home
June 1987

"Kendra, come on downstairs. Someone's here to see you."

I jumped up from my desk, finger-combed my hair into a loose pony tail and quickly changed from the frumpy, old T-shirt to the purple tank top Tommy liked. I thought he had to work today, but who else would be visiting?

I rushed to the bottom of the steps and ran smack dab into —"Mother?"

She wrapped her arms around me in a Giorgio-scented hug. I shrugged out of her embrace, and, backing away, glared at her.

"What are you doing here?"

Pa stepped to my side and touched my cheek. "Now, Kendra, that's no way to speak to your m—"

"My what? Mother? She stopped being that six years ago. You two go ahead and have a sweet little reunion. I want no part of it."

I shoved the back-porch screen door open so hard, it hit the house and swung wildly back, clipping my heel. Not slowing down, I ran blindly toward the sound. It didn't matter where I went as long as I got away.

I ended up at the wildlife refuge beside the creek throwing rock after rock into the water as hard as I could.

"Excuse me, miss. I have to ask you to stop throwing those rocks and scaring the fish and turtles."

I whipped one more rock in and turned my glare on...Tommy.

"I was on my way to your house with a surprise for you when you took off like there was a demon chasing you."

"It felt like there was." My whole body shook like a convulsion or something. And I was cold, so cold. I was what Pa called mad enough to spit bullets.

Tommy stepped in front of me. "Kenna, what's wrong? You haven't been this fired up about something since your Ma left."

"She came back."

"Who?"

"Mother waltzed right in the house happy to see me and all. Smothered me in a hug like she'd never deserted me. Her stinky perfume rubbed off on my clothes."

"Why do you think she came back after all these years?"

"I don't know, and I don't care."

I grabbed a handful of rocks and whooshed them into the creek. Did it again, throwing without thought or reason. The water that splashed on my face covered my tears.

Tommy grabbed my shoulder, and I shrugged him away. Didn't want comfort. Wanted to be angry. He stood beside me and waited.

"Kenna, I found this today and thought you might like to keep it on your desk." He pulled something out of his pocket and offered it to me.

A stupid rock? I grabbed it from his hand and whipped it into the creek where the water still rippled from my torrent.

"Rocks don't make me feel better."

Without missing a beat, Tommy walked straight into the creek and sloshed toward the spot where the rock had hit the water. Shoulders dropping, he turned to me.

"If you had looked at that one before throwing, it might have helped."

He picked up the rocks on the creek bottom and examined them. Felt like he searched forever. He even ducked his head under the water to look. How could he find one rock? Heck, the creek bed was nothing but rock.

Something in me snapped. There was my Tommy, fully clad, in the middle of the creek, picking up one rock after another, trying to find a specific one. Poor guy, got buzzed by dragonflies, pinched by crawfish, injured by dropped rocks that smashed his fingers, and he kept searching.

"You can stop looking."

"Ain't no way. I found that rock for you, and I aim to give it to you if I have to stay in this creek all day. You just sit there and watch me."

So I did. Then I started giggling. My big, strong, tough hunk of a boyfriend was picking up rocks like a kid.

"I found it! And a turtle too!"

He ran out of the water, holding a turtle in his left hand and the treasure rock in his right. Water dribbled off him and all over me when he sat on the ground beside me. Shaking his head like a dog sprayed water in my face.

He placed the turtle on the grass beside us. "I think the thing caught the rock, cuz it was on his back. Thanks, buddy."

The turtle ambled back toward the creek.

"Here, Kenna. I found this last weekend when I was camping with the guys. Soon's I saw it, I knew God made it for you. See? It looks just like a heart."

He handed me the rock. I closed my fingers around it and held it to my chest.

"I love it."

He smiled. "Then all of this was worth it. I want you to keep the rock forever, because my love for you will always be as solid as this rock."

He leaned in and gave me one of his melt-my-heart kisses.

Home
Present

Kendra looked at the girls. She tossed the rock up and caught it.

"You know, when I found out he was marrying Samantha, I tried to destroy this thing. I hit it with a sledge hammer and that little chip there on the side is all that happened. I threw it in the box. Figured so much for him loving me forever."

"But you kept it anyway. You still had hope, didn't you?" Adrienne slurped the last of her stew.

"We will always be special to each other. First love and all that. Life just took us different directions."

Kendra walked across the room to her desk and set the rock beside her journals. "I think I will keep it here from now on."

They started clearing the table and Arielle stopped at the desk. She touched the rock. "I like the chip in it. Gives it more character."

She pushed it further on the desk which bumped the stack of mail. Letters and bills scattered across the floor.

Arielle scooped them up and flipped through the envelopes. She lifted the attorney's letter "Momma, what's this?"

CHAPTER SIX

THE LETTER

Kendra made a grab for the letter. "It's nothing, just more attorney stuff."

Arielle held firm.

Kendra grumbled. If this was God's way of making sure she meant what she said about no more secrets, it wasn't funny. She planned to wait to tell them about this development until she had more details If only she'd tucked the letter into the bottom of the drawer.

Arielle skimmed over the letter and then passed it to Adrienne.

Both girls' faces registered the same disbelief as when they learned there was no Santa Claus. Kendra retrieved the letter, carefully folded it and slid it into the mail slot on the desk.

"Right now, that letter is all there is. Speculation. Nothing else. Remember when I told you the sheriff was baffled by your father's accident? He kept shaking his head and saying it didn't make sense. I guess he put that in the report. Now it's an investigation."

"Momma, who'd want to get back at Dad so bad they'd cause an accident?"

"Beats me. I'm sure the detective will visit me sometime and update me or question me or whatever it is he does. Accident or not, your father is still dead, and we still have to figure out what our 'next' looks like." Her shoulders dropped. "No, you two already have your next lined up. I have to figure out what mine is." Adrienne frowned.

"How hard this must be for you. I wonder—would it make things easier or more difficult right now if there weren't the Tommy complications?"

"They'd surely be different, but nothing makes losing a loved one easy. Girls, you must not forget that I did love Stan."

And she had. They weathered many years. Now he was gone. But violently murdered? Her knees buckled as she fell backwards into the desk chair. She hunched over and rested her head in her hands. His smiles when they explored new places... his laughter ... his joy when the girls were born...his strong arms holding her sometimes. Closing her eyes she squeezed back the tears that threatened. If she started she might never stop. Despite his short-comings, he was still a human being. He was still her husband and their father.

"He—he didn't deserve to be murdered."

Arielle rubbed her shoulders. "No, he didn't."

Adrienne retrieved the letter and read it again. "I think you should call the sheriff. Find out where the investigation is and offer to help. It would sure be better than wondering each day if you're in danger."

"You're right. I'll call first thing in the morning."

Kendra hung up and stared at the doodle-covered tablet. Not flowers and squiggles. These were angular, sharp. Angry doodles all around the notes she'd taken.

Stan's brake lines had multiple holes.

The car was going to crash with whoever drove it next.

Somebody knew Stan was leaving after that meeting and

driving over that bridge. But what if one of the girls had taken the car instead of him? Chills slid up her back.

If Stan had been faithful, so many things about their life would have been different, better. But someone had murdered him. Why?

She carried the trash can of various bottles out to the recycling can and threw them in, one at a time. Something about the breaking glass landing in the bin provided a needed outlet for venting.

After filling a trash can with broken bottles and jars, she could handle sorting through the information Sheriff Mitchell had given her. The funds from Stan's part of the brokerage were being held. Something about some suspicions Stan had about his partner's activities.

Kendra chewed on the end of her pen. Her husband had been a shrewd businessman and honest to a fault. His partner had been totally faithful to his wife but shady in business dealings. Between them they didn't even make a good man. Now one of them was dead and the other in trouble, possibly responsible for the death.

She bit the pen until it cracked. Her clenched her fists pounded the table so loud Arthur yipped. She needed a walk.

Kendra headed onto Main Street then beyond it to Ocean Drive. The vacant lots where houses had been last year before Irene swept up the coast saddened her.

Some houses were being rebuilt while other lots were just growing over. It reminded her of the day Aunt Susan had the city bring in bulldozers to hold her house up long enough for her to go in and get her china and precious things. Then they dozed it down. Aunt Susan had chosen not to rebuild.

Kendra stopped at the quaint bungalow on stilts that had weathered probably more storms than her house. It sported a fresh coat of paint and new supports beneath it to brace it for the next hurricane season. Really? Of all the directions she could have walked, this was the one she absently took. Or maybe it was intentional.

The shutters were open. A red Camaro was parked under the house and Creedence blared from the open living room window. Tommy was home.

Her heart beat a crazy rhythm. Part of her was hungry for one look at him, one chance to see him walk out onto the porch. But she wasn't ready. Not yet.

She turned toward home and ran as fast as her flip flops allowed.

The sheriff's car was parked at the curb as Kendra turned in. She shoved the car in park before stopping all the way and it lurched and stalled.

"Well, this day just gets better and better." She smoothed the wrinkles in her old T-shirt, finger combed loose hair back into the braid, and stomped sand from her feet.

The sheriff got out of his car.

"Hello, Kendra. It's been a long time."

Yeah, since he offered to help her in any way he could after her father died.

"Hey. I thought we covered things on the phone a while ago?"

He looked at the ground. "I thought we did too. Then I got a call from the mainland police. They were right ticked at me for not questioning you about Stan's—um—partner, Mr. Laurence."

Oh great.

"Would you maybe have a few minutes?"

No. "Sure. Come on in I'll make some coffee."

They entered the house.

"Have a seat. I'll be right back."

Kendra hustled to the kitchen and started the coffee, then

scooted upstairs to warn the girls. Heaven forbid if that they should come down in their pj's while the sheriff was there.

"Adrienne, Arielle? I just want you to know Sheriff Mitchell is here."

Rumbles greeted her. Typical. Those two might not be downstairs before lunch.

"The coffee's on."

More rumbles.

The coffeemaker beeped as she returned to the kitchen.

"Help yourself, Sheriff."

He ambled to the doorway. "Kendra, we've known each other since kindergarten. Just call me Bob."

"Okay, Bob. I wasn't sure since this is an official visit you'd be okay with casual."

She poured them each a mug and set them on the table. "Cream and sugar are on the counter if you need any."

"No need." He sat down across from her. "So, what can you tell me about TJ Laurence?"

She shuddered. "Not much. I never liked him. Stan kept all of his business matters to himself." Just like his personal matters. "He never even shared income information with me. I was quite shocked by the life insurance and what the will left to Adrienne, Arielle, and me. Of course, now it appears we won't get it anyway."

"I am sorry about that. Once the auditors do their jobs and the investigators theirs, it will be disbursed. Are you going to be all right till then?"

"I've got my own income. I don't know what to say about TJ. He was a staunch investor. He always came off as arrogant and overconfident to me. Could hardly stand to be around him."

"I see." Bob jotted some notes on his pad. "You wouldn't happen to know where he is now, would you?"

"Um, no. Ask his wife."

"They both disappeared three weeks after Stanton's funeral.

No one has heard from them at all. Their bank accounts were closed before they left. Did your husband have a safe here at the beach house?"

"No. Why?"

"We found some incriminating notes on TJ's desk. And a memo to get into Stanton's safe— but the rest was blurred by a water stain."

This was beyond understanding. Something nagged at the back of her mind. Something she should remember. But right now she couldn't recall the last time Stan even mentioned business to her.

Kendra chewed on her bottom lip. "We've never had a safe—"

She opened the top desk drawer and rifled through it. "Are you sure the note said a safe? Because about three years ago, Stan told me he had to open a safe deposit box here on the island. It was something about needing to keep some paperwork from TJ. I remember thinking how strange that was and wondering why he bothered to tell me. I have no clue where he put the key."

Bob finished his coffee and cleared his throat. "Kendra, I need you to remember." He pulled a card from his pocket. "Call me as soon as you find that key. Okay?"

She took the card.

"I will."

She closed the door as he got in his car and drove away. Leaning against the back door, she slid to the floor.

"Oh Stanton, how many messes did you have yourself in?"

CHAPTER SEVEN

MIMOSA FLOWER

*K*endra leaned back against the door. She picked at the polish on her nails. "You cheated on me over and over and I was too insecure to leave. You knew that didn't you. I just enabled you all those years. Then you died. But now they tell me it was not an accident and your partner is the key suspect. What am I supposed to do with all of this? Tell me Stan. Oh yeah, you can't."

She stared at her fingers and then brushed the nail polish chips into her palm. "Yes, I am picking my nails again. Oh how you hated that. But you're not here to fuss at me now."

She pounded clenched fists on the floor and swore.

Bedroom doors opened and Adrienne beat Arielle down.

"What's going on, Mom?" She stopped punching and rubbed her hands together. Ouch.

Arielle knelt beside her and grasped Kendra's hand. "Oh my goodness, look at your hand. It's all red and swollen."

"I think I've reached my limit on what I can deal with at one time."

"Adrienne, get some ice. Momma, does this have something to do with the sheriff's visit?"

"Yeah, but it's not his fault." She started to sniff. "It's just... well...something about money...and Mr. Laurence...and a key... and ... oh, it's all a big mess."

Adrienne wrapped Kendra's knuckles in icy cold towels. "I think they will be all right. Sore, but all right. Why don't you go get some air? It'll clear your head. You'll feel better."

"You're probably right. Beating myself up surely isn't doing me any good." She trudged to the door then paused. "Thanks you two. What would I do without you? I'll be okay. Have your breakfast or lunch whichever it is at this time of day. I won't be gone long."

Kendra raced to the old tree, slid to the grass underneath, and leaned her head against it. She rubbed her sore knuckles. Why did things have to be so difficult? Four years ago Pa would have dropped whatever project he was working on and sat beside her until she was okay. But that would never happen again.

"Oh, Pa, I miss you. I could sure use your wisdom right now."

A breeze tickled her face.

A blossom dislodged by the wind floated down and landed in her lap. She picked up the wispy flower and feathered it on her cheek.

"Thanks, Pa, but it's not the same. I need you here to help me know what to do and say."

She gathered a handful of flowers from the ground.

Maybe talking about the flowers and Pa was how he could help her through this day. She went back inside. The turtle box was in it honorary place in the center of the doily on the table. She spread the flowers around it. They would wilt quickly, but they'd still be pretty.

Adrienne sat at the desk, writing, and Arielle was across the room, sewing her new blouse. Kendra poured a mug of coffee and sat at the table.

"When you two are ready for a break, I'm over my tantrum." She opened the box. "Are you okay?"

Adrienne closed her notebook. "It's like you said yesterday, it's nothing until it's something. We don't have to fix it, we can't fix it. We have to wait. And we'll wait together."

"How'd you get so wise?"

Arielle laughed. "I taught her."

"Seriously Mom, there's really nothing we can do. If you're up for it another story might be the perfect diversion."

"Couldn't hurt to try."

Like eager children, both of them jumped from their projects and hustled to the table.

Arielle picked up a flower. "I remember you used to put these flowers in little bowls all over the house in the summer."

Kendra offered them the laminated one.

"I told you we're doing things in order. Even though it's like losing your place in a book and reading two chapters ahead before you realize it, now's a good time to share this one. This is the only thing in the box that isn't from Tommy. It's from Pa."

They passed it between them with a gentle reverence.

"In some ways I mourned this the most when your father told me he'd thrown the box away. This flower was the last thing Pa gave me before he died. I had only placed it in the box earlier that day when Stan took the box."

Adrienne leaned back in her chair and stretched her long legs under the table, bumping Kendra's feet. Arielle rested her chin in her hands on the table.

"I love mimosa trees. They smell so pretty when they're blooming. On a breezy day the wispy pink flowers look like they're dancing on the branches."

She reached to the center of the table and ran her fingers across the tips of the flowers.

"As much as I loved the trees, Mother hated them. She called them dirty. If she'd had her way about it, Pa would've chopped them down. Even though the whole town is named after them. Funny thing is, he usually did everything she asked of him. But he wouldn't cut the tree down. He'd say, "Now, Miss Marie, I'd do pert' near anything you asked of me. But our little Kendra loves the flowers on that tree. And as long as I am able, I will keep one of those trees in our yard for her.'"

"Oh, Mother was mad. That may be the only time in their marriage he didn't give her what she wanted."

Arielle puffed her bangs from her face. "They were such an odd couple. We were the only kids at school whose grandparents could live separate lives and still be together. Grams was always off on some whirlwind tour or making one of her books into a movie, and Papa was always here. How did they ever get together?"

Kendra smiled. "He swept her off her feet when they were both in college. They fell crazy in love, from what I was told. That love never died. Never. It's just that Mother's career came first. Pa was willing to wait for her. I wasn't."

Adrienne pursed her lips and snorted. "Hardly seems fair."

"What part of life is? I know when she came home sick and he got to take care of her those last few years, he was doing what he wanted to do more than anything in the world."

"Was that hard for you?"

Kendra doodled circles on the table wither finger. "It was good to see Pa happy again. And for the first time in my life, Mother was actually gentle with me. I knew Pa wouldn't live a long time after she died. I think the only reason he lasted four years was because of you two and me."

Kendra put the sealed flower on top of the box.

"Pa started picking one flower each morning and setting it on my dresser so I would see it when I got up. It got so special to me that when the tree stopped blooming that year, I cried.

"The next summer, as soon as the tree flowered he started bringing one to me every day. But he also gathered them, flattened them, and then froze them to preserve the color. The last step was sealing them in wax paper. I had no idea what he was up to."

Kendra wiped her eyes.

"He hid them from me all summer. And when the tree dropped its last flower, he had a supply of them stored away. Until the day he went to the hospital, I had a flower for every day of the year."

Arielle was crying. "But, Momma, you didn't live here forever. What did he do, mail them to you?"

She nodded. "When I moved away, he took to freezing them in a zipper bags. He mailed me a bag each week."

"And that's why you had the bowl of dried flowers on your dresser?" Arielle asked.

"Yes. His last day, he picked the first blossom of the summer, placed it on my dresser, then went downstairs and had the stroke.

"After his funeral, I couldn't bear to look at the tree. I went into the shed and got the axe. The only reason this tree remains is because Tommy followed me home. He said he saw Stan get into his car and zoom away as soon as the graveside service was done and didn't think I should be alone. When he got here, I was picking up the axe. He grabbed the handle and suggested I give it a few months and if I still wanted it down by Christmas, he would chop it down for me." She looked out the door at the tree. "By Christmas I couldn't think of chopping it down."

"Thank God Tommy followed you."

"Yes." Kendra picked up the flower and held it to her heart. "The last thing Pa ever did was make sure his girl had her morning flower."

CHAPTER EIGHT

KEY AND CONFESSION

Home
Present

Kendra stared out the back door at the rain pelting the bay. It matched her mood of the past few days. She'd snapped at pretty much anyone who crossed her path. Which meant Arthur and the girls took the brunt of it.

Trying to drag herself out of her funk, she wandered about the house, straightening and organizing. Well, that was what she told herself she was doing. Mostly, she just moved things from one stack to another. If she didn't watch out, she'd end up like Aunt May, filling a house with unending piles of things she might need or use sometime.

She rolled the old desktop closed with a bang. Maybe she could tackle another task.

With folded linens in hand, Kendra headed upstairs. She opened the door to the room she and Stan shared whenever he managed to get away from work—or whatever—and spend a weekend with them. His closet was still full, his dresser too. Going through this stuff and boxing presented an opportunity for constructive venting.

Or crying.

Or ripping the clothes to shreds.

Or whatever she wanted to do.

She leaned against the door jamb and puffed a stray piece of hair out of her eyes.

Adrienne stepped into the hallway. "What's up, Mom?"

"I'm all scattered this morning. But I think it's time to tackle this room. Maybe getting it empty will help. If all three of us work together, we can have it done by lunch."

Adrienne cocked her head to one side. "Are you sure that's what you want to do? I mean, your mood has not been the best this week."

Blunt, but truthful.

"Actually, I'm sure it's what I don't want to do. But I do want the room cleared. Plus, I promised Bob we'd look for the key."

"Okay then. Let me get Arielle's lazy butt out of bed. We can help."

Within an hour of starting the process, things looked hopeless. Every available surface had clothing—stacks to give to Goodwill and stacks to throw away. A mountain of coat hangers piled in the corner resembled some sort of abstract wire-and-plastic sculpture. While the unused boxes waited just inside the doorway.

Only a small pathway was open from the hallway through the room. So, when Adrienne returned from filling their water bottles, Arthur circled around her feet making her stumble into the boxes. Arielle tried to help but tripped over a dresser leg sending the shirts in her arms flying.

Kendra wished she could have seen it all in slow motion. Legs, arms, water bottles, boxes, and shirts scattered. One daughter landed on the other and she burst into laughter.

"If only I'd had my phone ready. This was not your most graceful of moments."

Arielle kicked a box off her legs. "At least we did it together."

"In true twin form." Kendra moved a couple of boxes. "You should have seen your faces."

"Hey Momma, give me a hand here."

When Kendra reached for Arielle her daughter pulled her into the pile with her.

Laughter. Unabashed laughter.

Kendra climbed out of the box pile and examined the mess they'd made. "I think we need a better plan. Let's forget making stacks. Why not just fold the clothes and pack them directly into boxes. But keep looking for that safe deposit key too. "

She stood in the middle of the chaos and scratched her head. "The thing is, he mentioned it in passing one night when we were here. I never thought to ask why he'd rented the box or where the key was."

Kendra looked around the room and sighed. "I guess we have to go through every pocket, every shoebox, everything."

Arielle opened a dresser drawer. "Maybe he just had it tucked back in a corner like your turtle box."

"We can hope. I'll take the closet shelves. Arielle, you do the dresser and chest of drawers; Adrienne can do the shoes and his desk."

"Sounds like a plan." They spoke together.

They worked until late morning. Once they'd boxed the clothes and pushed them into the hallway, they moved more easily around the room. By the time the closet was empty, each of them sported one of Stan's suit jackets and had various ties wrapped around their necks like scarves.

"Oh, Momma, remember this tie? I picked the loud fabric and made it in home ec. I was so proud of myself." Arielle wrapped it around her head like a headband. "I can't believe he actually wore it to work the next day."

Adrienne pulled out a pair of toe socks. "Oh gracious, he still had these? We were like seven when we gave these to him for Christmas. He wore them every day during that holiday."

Kendra smiled. It was healthy to think of the good times too.

"Remember how you two always hid from him when he got home from work? The day you managed to get on top of the cabinets, I about had a heart attack when I saw you up there."

They sat on the floor and looked around the empty room.

"Is that everything?"

Then Kendra looked at the dresser and closet. "It's all empty?"

"Yep," they spoke together.

"Is it okay that I miss him?" Arielle rubbed the brim of Stan's hat. "I mean, I think I could be mad at him forever for pretty much everything. But he was my daddy."

Kendra removed the hat she wore. She ran her fingers around the rim, lifted it to her nose and sniffed the lingering scent of his conditioner. She blew her breath out in one slow puff.

"Of course you miss him. I do too."

They removed their attire and shoved it into the last box.

The room was now void of any vestige of her dead husband's existence. All reminders of him packed away. Surveying the boxes that surrounded her, she rejected the idea that a person's life could be reduced to the contents of a few boxes. There was more to life than that.

"Everything that seems so important in life—the things you spend money on and cherish—in the end get reduced to just a bunch of boxes." Kendra sat on the edge of the bed.

Twenty-seven years was a long time. And now he was gone. Just gone. What if she had confronted him about things. Could he have changed? Would he have changed? Maybe it was her fault, after all. If she'd been more into the high society, elite circles, maybe he wouldn't have looked for other women.

No, this wasn't productive. She used to beg him to get counseling, or to move away, or to take more weekends away with her so they could reconnect. He was always too busy and counseling was a waste of money as far as he was concerned. Things could have been so much better. But even if they had been, he'd still be dead and all parts of him boxed and stacked.

Kendra grabbed a throw pillow and hugged it to her chest. "Oh Stan."

Adrienne began moving the boxes into the hallway as Arielle worked on closing closets and drawers. One of the dresser drawers was jammed. She pushed and pulled until one good hard jerk freed the drawer landing her on her butt on the floor.

Giggles erupted.

Arielle stood and tried to replace it into the dresser, then she stopped. After examining the sides and bottom she removed another drawer and did the same thing.

"Momma?"

"What is it?"

"Someone painted arrows all inside these drawers."

"What?"

"Come see. There are random arrows pointing all different directions in both of them." After showing them to Kendra, she put them on the floor and slid out another. "And this one too. What in the world? There's numbers too. It's like a dresser drawer treasure map. Don't see an X yet, though."

"Well I did get this at a yard sale. Your dad was indignant I would buy second-hand until I told him I just wanted it here for his clothes. I never paid much attention to it. I would just put his clothes in it and shut the drawers. Let me have a look."

Kendra walked across the room. Sure enough, arrows pointing out some weird pattern in all of the drawers. "I bet some kid painted them. But really, girls, we have enough to worry about, don't we?"

Reluctantly, Arielle replaced drawers and shoved the dresser back against the wall.

Kendra grabbed the box closest to the door and hefted it up.

"What say we haul these downstairs, then take a break on the porch?"

"I like that plan." Adrienne picked up a box and followed. She stopped at the top of the steps and turned back. "Arielle, are you coming?"

"In a minute."

🐢

Kendra and Adrienne sat on the porch steps, sipping mint tea and watching Arthur chase butterflies until thumping and bumping noises coming from upstairs interrupted.

"I thought she said she'd be right down. What in the world prompted her to rearrange now?"

"She's not in her room, Mom. That's coming from Dad's room. We better check."

"Come on, Arthur." Kendra held the door for the pup then followed Adrienne upstairs.

They froze in the doorway. The dresser was pulled away from the wall and all of the drawers were scattered on the floor upside down or sideways. Arielle sat amidst the disorder, grinning like a Cheshire cat. She opened her palm, showing them a key.

Kendra stepped into the room. "What on earth?"

"It was in that drawer."

"Which one?"

"The one with the most arrows. You know me. I couldn't walk away without trying to figure out what they were all about. So I started with the one on the inside front of the drawer. It was crazy trying to follow them, but they worked their way back to the first one. The last arrow pointed to this key taped in the upper corner of the dresser."

Adrienne took the key.

"It sure looks like a safe-deposit-box key." She examined it and handed it to Kendra.

"Why in the world would my particularly, type-A husband choose this method to hide it?"

"Because no one would expect it. They'd figure a kid did it, just like we did. Good work Arielle."

Kendra closed the key in her palm. What was it Stan had said that day he told her about the box? Snippets of the memory trickled to her.

"It was for me. When he came back from the bank the day he opened the safe-deposit box, he told me he'd opened one for work. I asked him why here instead of Richmond where the business was.

"He set his jaw and said it was all work stuff. Nothing I needed to worry about. He walked out of the room, then turned back and said something about if I ever needed to find it all I had to do was follow the arrows."

She rubbed her hands together.

"He'd already had several drinks that night. I thought he was talking nonsense. It appears he wasn't."

"What do we do with it, Momma?"

"I told the sheriff I'd give it to him. And I will. But first I want to see what's in it. I don't want any more surprises."

"Can we go with you? You probably shouldn't do this alone."

"Actually, I need to. I'll head out in a little while and see what's in the box. Then I'll give the key to the sheriff and be back for a late lunch."

Kendra stared across the yard into the sound. The tide was out, and a walk on the shore in the rain would be soothing about now. But she promised Bob, and if she put this off, it would eat away at her nerves.

Might as well get this over with. She grabbed her keys and purse and rushed through the downpour to her car.

"Mrs. Michaels, everyone here at Sands Bank is sorry for your loss. Stanton Michaels was a good man."

Sometimes. She faced the bank manager.

"Thank you, sir."

Mr. Jones escorted her into the vault. He inserted his key into the lock, and she followed suit. He removed the drawer and pointed down a short corridor.

"The second door on the right is the viewing room. Take as long as you like. The door locks automatically for privacy, but you can open it from inside." He placed the drawer on the desk and left the room.

In the room, Kendra sat on the cold metal chair. A chill colder than the chair chased up her spine. She reached to open the lid, but stopped. This little metal box was about to undo her composure.

From the recesses of her mind, she heard Pa. "Now Kendra Lynn Thomas, there are no monsters under that bed except for the ones your mind put there. I just read you a stack of books, and I'm tired. You go on in that room. If something scares you, I promise to come the second you call."

And he always had.

She looked to the ceiling and hoped somehow Pa was still protecting her from whatever monsters lurked in the box.

She opened it.

It was filled with manila envelopes, folders, and one smaller, letter-sized envelope addressed to her. In twenty-seven years marriage, the man had never written her a letter. Something told her this one would be important.

She pushed her finger under the seal and slid it across. Ouch! Paper cut. She stuck the finger in her mouth.

Dang. The man could dish out pain even beyond the grave. Trembling hands removed the letter from the envelope and unfolded the yellow legal paper. How he loved his legal pads. She got him a stack of blue ones once which he refused to use. She remembered threatening to buy pink ones next time. His eyes had shot daggers at her.

Kendra sighed. The letter was dated three years ago. He must have put it in there the day he rented the box.

Dear Kendra,

If you are reading this, then you followed the arrows, found the key, you're sitting in the quiet room—and I am dead.

I'm sorry for everything.

Everything.

I knew when I married you that your heart was—and would always be—divided. I slammed you about Tommy as often as I could to assuage my own guilt for my constant infidelities. I could lie to myself and say I will change my ways, but even as I sit here writing this, I am not alone.

Kendra dropped the letter on the table.

Jerk.

She shoved the box across the table. It hit the floor with a noise like a gunshot. Files and papers scattered everywhere.

Mr. Jones spoke through the door. "Mrs. Michaels, are you all right?"

"I'm fine." She yelled at the closed door.

Leaving the papers on the floor, she continued reading.

So, again I say I am sorry.

In this box are all of the files the sheriff needs. He's probably already shown up, asking you about the box. TJ's
embezzling from Dad's company and setting me up for the
fall. As soon as I figured this out, I hired another accoun-
tant on the side, and he's been documenting everything.

I plan to turn TJ in once I get all the information compiled.
I don't want him to get off scot-free. But, since you're
reading this, my plan probably failed. Be careful. If TJ
thinks you know anything ...well, just be careful.

Kendra, thank you for being the wife I never deserved and
the perfect mother. As much as my selfish heart could, I did
love you.

If there is anything about this life I know, it is that you
deserve to be loved fully, completely, perfectly. Go to
Tommy. You two need each other.

Please take the contents of the box to the sheriff. No matter
what, make that your next stop.

Loving regards,
Stan

p.s. Your turtle box is in the far back corner of my closet.
I'm sorry I took it. Of all the lies I've told you, I'm glad I
lied about breaking that box.

The letter fluttered to the floor.

Kendra pushed the chair out of the way so she could retrieve
the papers, files and envelopes. Holding her tote open, she shoved

them inside. Three years the man knew about this and never bothered to tell her? How much at risk had he put her and the girls?

She whipped her phone open and dialed Sheriff Mitchell.

"Hello?"

"Hey, it's Kendra Michaels. I just cleared out the safe-deposit box and have a bag full of files for you. I'm on—"

A text beeped in. She stared at it. Her hands shook hard enough she lost her grip on the phone.

A distant voice called, "Kendra? Are you still there?"

After wiping her wet palms on her jeans, she picked it up. "Dropped the phone. Umm, Bob, Arielle just texted me. TJ Laurence has been calling all morning. Adrienne and Arielle have not answered it."

Through the phone Kendra heard what sounded like a chair slam against a desk and keys jingling. "Tell them I'm on my way and they should probably leave. Meet me at the end of your road. Do not go home without me."

Yeah right. "I'll meet you in my drive, Bob. I have to be sure they are gone."

His phone clicked off.

"Lord, help us."

Kendra sped home. Arielle's car was gone. At least they took Bob's advice. She would just go inside real quick and maybe check to see if TJ left a message, then she'd go back and meet Bob.

CHAPTER NINE

THE ARREST

Kendra parked her Jeep in the drive and took a deep breath. Was this a good idea? Pursing her lips and clearing her throat she walked to the front door. She'd only be here a few minutes.

Before she closed the door she heard heavy footsteps on the porch. TJ crossed from the porch swing to stand beside her.

"Hey, Kendra. I've been calling for a while. No one answered so I figured you were away. Decided to come and wait. The girls raced out the back door and drove away like a bat outta hell about ten minutes ago. Everything okay?"

"I don' know. As you can see, I just got home."

Breathe. Speak slowly. Act normal.

"It's good to see you, TJ. How've you been?"

"I'm dealing. You?"

"Same."

Stopping in the doorway, she turned to him. "I was only coming in to check my laundry before heading back out. Can we chat another time?"

"I'd rather talk right now, if you don't mind. I am on a schedule. He walked passed her into the house. He walked right into the kitchen and turned a chair backwards before straddling it. His knees bounced like a jack hammer, and he continued running his hands through his hair. This man was about to lose it. Kendra wasn't sure how long he'd hold on.

Leaving the front door open, she dropped her purse on the desk and joined him in the kitchen. "TJ, you look like a stress ball. Would you like a glass of mint tea?"

"I-I could use some. Thanks."

She put ice in a large glass, filled it with tea then set it before him. Hopefully, Bob would arrive soon.

The kitchen was charged with tension like air with electricity before an electrical storm. TJ's hands trembled so much tea sloshed out of the glass when he drank. Wild eyes glared at her.

Kendra plastered on her best sympathetic smile.

"I haven't seen you since the funeral. How have you been?"

"It's hard, Kendra. Mr. Michaels is stalling with the paperwork to turn the business over to me. Evidently, he has more input into the board's decisions than I do, even though Stan and I were supposed to be equal partners. Feels like they're trying to get rid of me. That's tough on top of losing Stan."

"I'm sure it is."

How could this man sound so honest and sincere? If she hadn't just read Stan's letter, she'd have believed everything TJ was saying. Maybe Stan's father knew and was biding his time. Another Michaels man placing her and her daughters in danger.

God help her. Sitting in the kitchen, drinking tea with the man who probably murdered her husband was insane. *Hurry up, Bob.*

Peering over her glass, she encountered TJ's disconcerting wild-eyed glare. She had to keep him talking. Keep him calm. Before she could think of something to say, he finished his tea and slammed the glass onto the table so hard it broke in his hand.

"Look, Kendra, we could sit here and share niceties all afternoon, but it wouldn't change things. You've got something I need."

"What in the world are you talking about?"

"You're no actress, so don't bother playing coy with me. Stan told me you could never lie, not even to keep a surprise party a secret. So, why don't you just tell me where the key is?"

He glared at her.

"I don't know—"

"You know exactly what I mean. And I hope for your sake you haven't used it yet. Give me the key to Stan's safe-deposit box." He held out his hand to her.

"What use do I have for it? Stan told me it was all business stuff. I know right where it is."

She walked to the desk, opened the middle drawer and rummaged around in it. A car door closed. "I know it's in here somewhere." Hopefully, she made enough noise to cover the outside ones.

With one hard push, she shoved the drawer and removed the key from her shirt pocket. Turning toward TJ, she offered the key to him. "Here it is. I hope this is what you're looking for."

He grabbed the key from her and rushed to the front door just as Bob walked inside. "What's your hurry, Mr. Laurence?"

TJ turned and raced past her, back to the kitchen and right into a large state trooper entering the back door.

In a matter of minutes, they had TJ handcuffed and escorted to the police car. Bob tipped his hat to her. "I'll be in touch, but from what I scanned quickly, the tote bag in your car contained everything we need to convict him of embezzlement and probably Stanton's death too."

Words escaped her. She watched the cars leave and trudged back to the table. She pulled the turtle box to her and absently began picking up treasures and dropping them back inside.

Adrienne and Arielle returned after the sheriff and state police drove away. Kendra was still at the table, rolling the tiny shell around in her hand.

Adrienne busied herself making hot chocolate, and Arielle sat across from Kendra. She grasped her hand.

"A penny for your thoughts, Momma?"

Kendra pulled her hand free and tapped the shell on the table before dropping it.

"I'm just so angry at Stanton. If he had turned TJ in when he first suspected something, he wouldn't have placed all of us in danger."

"And he'd still be alive."

Unspoken misery filled the silence between them.

If her husband walked in the door and stood in front of her right this moment, she'd slug him. But he wouldn't. And she was stuck here trying to figure things out on her own. Her vision blurred and tremors shook her. She watched her hands close into fists as if they were not even part of her body. She jumped up from the table and rushed to the door. Before stepping outside, she faced them.

"Give me a few minutes, okay?"

"If you're gone too long, Momma, we're coming to get you."

Adrienne nodded.

Kendra had slumped onto the top step of the porch before the door banged shut. She rested her head in her hands, closed her eyes and thanked God for their safety.

Arielle opened the screen a crack, and Arthur scooted into Kendra's lap. "The little guy needs you as much as you need him. We've got the broken glass cleaned up. Hot chocolate's ready. Do you want it out here or inside with us?"

She nuzzled Arthur's fur. "We'll be in shortly."

As Kendra watched a lone sailboat on the bay, she lost track of time. It might have been a few minutes or maybe even an hour. She wasn't sure which. But, she told them she'd be in shortly and

Arthur had already squirmed out of her lap and was racing around the yard.

"Come on, buddy, let's go in."

Arielle and Adrienne were on the floor on either side of the coffee table, sipping hot chocolate and playing their family game, mancala. She joined them. As soon as she sat, Adrienne closed the game and handed Kendra a mug.

"Mom, have some chocolate therapy. This stuff is good for what ails you."

"True enough."

Kendra took a sip of the hot goodness and got a drop of whipped cream on her nose. They all chuckled. A little laughter in this tense day felt nice. She glanced around the room.

"You cleaned up."

"We had to do something to burn the nervous energy. I dusted and Arielle vacuumed. Didn't you hear us?"

"No. I wasn't hearing much of anything. Took forever for the trembling to stop. I'm not used to these panic attacks. They come on so quickly and then just end. Maybe now they will stop since the whole thing with TJ is over."

"Mom, it's not really over. There will be questions and court and lawsuits and all kinds of junk. TJ really messed with us, and Dad. Who wasn't much help either. You're right, he put us in danger by keeping his suspicions secret like that. It makes me mad. I even checked to see if you left any bottles for me to break like you did the other day."

Arielle finished her mug. "I'm a mess about all of this. I'm sad he died. I'm mad at so much of what he did. I'm really ticked at how much he hurt you for so long. And, I have to admit, I don't fully understand why you stayed with him."

"I've always told myself I stayed for you two. Maybe I did. I'm pretty sure it's called codependence. But it's always easy to figure it out after the fact. I'll not beat myself up over the what-if's of my life anymore. If nothing else good ever comes out of this, I think I need to remember my past shaped my present, but it doesn't have to define my future. God's got control of that. Maybe it's time for me to try that recovery program at church."

"I might go with you, Mom," Arielle said.

"Me too." Adrienne opened the turtle box. "If it's okay with the two of you, I want to change the subject. If this day hadn't gone so crazy which thing would you have told us about next?"

Kendra retrieved the perfect little shell and placed it beside her mug. "Telling this might help, but I'm not sure I have it in me today. We'll get to it tomorrow."

The disappointment on Adrienne's face almost convinced her to change her mind. But hadn't she just said she wasn't going to live in the past? That included not doing something she didn't need to do because the girls might be unhappy.

"Today is the first day I try to be un-codependent, if that's a word. The old me would give in to you and tell the story. But the new me, the one I think I'm just introducing us all to right now, needs to wait until tomorrow."

They smiled and spoke together. "You go, girl."

CHAPTER TEN

THE PROMISE SHELL

*K*endra was on her third and final cup of coffee when she heard her daughters grumbling their way down the stairs. Without a word, they poured themselves a mug of coffee.

Adrienne spoke first. "Hey."

"Hey yourself. How late were you two out last night? I never heard you come in."

"I was ready to come home by midnight, but the life of the party over there was having too much fun doing karaoke."

Arielle sat on Kendra's other side, holding her mug in one hand and a cream-filled doughnut with the other. Crumbs dropped out as she spoke. "You lie. It wasn't me. Everyone was shocked at how Adrienne got up there and let loose. She's always the reasonable one. And no, Adrienne wasn't drunk. None of us was drinking. I kept asking her who she was and what she'd done with my sister."

"After the day we had, I needed to let go a little bit. I'd do it again." She dragged the turtle box from the center of the table and placed it in front of her. After opening it, she picked up the little shell and rolled it in her hand. "I think you told us this one is the next story."

"I did. For the record, you're going to love this story."

They perked up.

"Tommy spent the weekend before he left for college here at Mimosa Beach. With me. Alone."

Arielle's eyes widened. "Mom! You? Really?"

Kendra's cheeks warmed. Yeah, this story was going to be fun, and a bit scandalous. She sipped her coffee, eyeing them over the rim of her mug.

"All teenagers do things they would never do as adults or want their children to know about. Present company included."

They sat straight and alert.

Home
August 1988

I watched Pa drive away. His relationship with Mother would forever remain a mystery to me. Humph. Mother. Since she stopped being my mommy years ago, I needed to give her a new name to make my point. "Mom" didn't fit, so I started calling her Mother. What was it she said when she'd visited last? Something about how sophisticated I'd grown. Like that was my goal in life.

Two days ago, she informed Pa she needed him to come to the mainland and fix a water leak in the house. Seriously? Last I knew, there were plumbers on the mainland. And she surely could afford to pay one. But no, she interrupted Pa at work, and he went running. I didn't get it. Not only did she mess up Pa's weekend plans, but mine too. So much for Tommy and me taking the boat over to Picnic Island our last weekend together before he left for college.

Pa gave me last minute instructions before he left. He was

quite clear about what he expected me to do. "Kendra, I trust you and will let you stay home this weekend. But there's no boating when I'm off the island. You and Tommy will have to make other plans."

I closed the door and spoke to the air. "Once again, Mother, you've ruined my plans. My life."

The back door opened, and Tommy breezed in. "Kenna, you here? You ready? I have the picnic packed. Let's go."

He stopped in the hallway. "Uh-oh. You have your 'mother look' on your face. What happened?"

"My what?"

"Ever since she came back into your life, when she does something that messes with you, you get this angry look, your 'mother look.' What did she do now?"

I sat down on the Parsons Bench in the foyer. Tommy sat beside me and grabbed my hand.

"Mother had a plumbing issue, and Pa went running as always. Doesn't he know she uses him?"

Tommy nodded. "Sure he does. But he's a strong man of faith and convictions. And he loves her." He brushed my hair out of my face. "He doesn't want us taking the boat out when he's off the island."

I nodded.

"Okay, then we go to the Preserve and hike back to our cove. It'll be more private there anyway. I wasn't real excited about sharing you with the gang out on Picnic Island today. The Preserve is closed this weekend, but Joe will let us in."

He made a good point.

"Kenna?" He grasped my chin and tilted my face up so I could look into those chocolate-brown eyes. "I want you all to myself today."

"I'd like that." My heart about beat its way right out of my chest. Then he kissed me. Oh my.

I ran upstairs, threw on my swimsuit and cover-up and then

braided my hair. Flip-flops in hand, I raced back to Tommy. He stood at the bottom of the steps, shaking his head.

"We got all day, girl. Don't hurt yourself."

I stopped in front of him and stood on tippy-toes for a kiss.

He kissed the tip of my nose. "I tell you, Kenna, I'm not sure I've ever seen you look prettier than when you ran downstairs just now. I think it beats the way you looked prom night."

Dang, that boy knew how to say the right things. My heart didn't stop its crazy drumbeat all day long.

🐢

Home
Present

Kendra noticed the morning rain had stopped and sunlight filtered through the lace curtains, casting spider-web shadows on the wall. But the living room was really the wrong place to tell the tiny shell story.

"Since the rain's stopped, we could go to the Preserve where this actually happened. Of all the times we've been there, I never took you to our spot. As soon as you get dressed, we'll head out."

"Momma, this is so romantic. It would be even more romantic if Tommy shows up while we're there."

"I'm not ready for that." She doubted he remembered anyway.

Adrienne blocked the doorway.

"I have to say this. If you get mad at me, well that's okay. But I am not going to tiptoe around it anymore."

Arielle rubbed her hands together as she plopped on the Parson Bench at the door.

Kendra looked from one daughter to the other. She recognized the look in their eyes. There was a plot amiss. She braced herself for whatever was coming.

Adrienne reached for her hand. "Mom, it's time for honesty,

not just with us, but also yourself. You're telling us these stories, and we love it. It makes us so happy to know you had such a sweet love in your life.

"But you need to cut yourself some slack. We loved Dad, and we miss him. It's okay that you don't. It's okay that you still love Tommy. You always taught us to believe in ourselves and to trust God has a plan for us. Do you believe your own words?"

Kendra nodded.

"Because Tommy may have been part of His plan for you all along. Maybe He's been waiting for some of these bad human choices to bring you around to this moment right now."

"Well, I—"

Arielle held her finger to her lips. "Shh!"

"Mom, all we want is for you to give God the opportunity to give you a second chance. Stop avoiding Tommy. We've been praying about this. Come out of that turtle shell Tommy talked about. It's okay for you to be happy."

Kendra was flabbergasted. She opened her mouth to reply, but nothing came. She slammed it closed.

"That's what I needed to say. If you're not mad, we can go to the Preserve now."

The Preserve
Present

Kendra stared across the marshland as the girls spread the quilt over the tarp. The ground was still wet from the morning deluge, but the air smelled of salt and summer.

She sat between them on the tarp. Her daughters had grown up to be stronger and wiser than she'd ever been. Though she had resented her mother for years, she'd never been brave enough to be honest with her. Never strong enough to speak with the boldness her daughters had.

Kendra looked from one to the other and then broke the silence. "Thank you for speaking truth to me."

Sighs released on either side of her. Adrienne spoke, "You're not mad?"

"I think you two have grown into wise women and I would do well to take your advice. I'm just not sure I can handle another betrayal."

"Where's your faith? You've always told us if it's God's plan, nothing can stop it—delay it maybe, but not stop it. You've already had the delay, Mom." Adrienne squeezed her hand.

"I'll think and pray on it. That's all I can do."

"That's all that's needed, Mom."

Arielle opened the box and retrieved the shell.

"So, tell us about this."

Kendra's hand closed around the shell. "I actually haven't been back here since I got this shell. That was a good day, one of the best ever. We came here for our picnic. The ranger let us in and told us we could have the whole Preserve to ourselves. Tommy grabbed my hand and about dragged me here."

The Preserve
August 1988

We ran out of the water hand in hand and dropped to Nana's quilt. Tommy lay on his side, propped his head up on one hand, while the other gently touched my cheeks, chin, and hair. He leaned toward me and kissed me softly at first, then deeper and more passionately. When he pulled away, I could hardly breathe.

"Kenna, I love you."

How I loved to hear him say those words.

"Pretty sure I always have. Going away is killing me. I don't give a damn about college or careers or anything if it takes me away from you. But I want to be able to provide for you. It's a conundrum."

I slid closer to him and snuggled in his arms. I didn't care what we did or where we lived as long as we were together.

"I love you too, Tommy."

He kissed the top of my head.

"I want to marry you, to spend my life with you. But I have college and you will too. Is it fair of me to ask you to wait that long?"

"Fair? I don't know. But what I do know, Tommy Leon King, is I will wait for you, and I will be your wife one day."

Tommy kissed me again. And again. I didn't want to stop, but he sat up.

"Kenna, not here. Let's take a walk."

He grabbed my hand and pulled me up. We walked through the marsh, then on the beach for hours. Talked about us and college and life and made all sorts of plans for the future.

"I bought the rings and wanted to give yours to you today. Dad put the kibosh on it. He says we're too young. I have to honor his wishes since he's paying for college. I'll hang onto them.

"You know I don't agree with him. Heck, he and Mom got married when they were nineteen. He reminded me they had both graduated. Says I at least have to wait until you graduate from high school."

I'd have felt much more secure with a ring on my finger during the year we were separated. But I couldn't tell him that. He looked so sad. "It's okay, Tommy. I think we just promised each other, didn't we?"

"Yep."

"That's good enough for me. You've never broken a promise to me."

He pulled me into my arms and held me tight as we watched

the sun set together one last time. When we turned to leave, he saw the shell. He picked it up and kissed it, then handed it to me. It was the most perfect little shell I'd ever seen.

"A promise shell. With this shell I promise you that one day I will marry you, Kendra Lynn Thomas."

"And I you, Thomas Leon King."

🐢

Present

Kendra stopped. Breathing was difficult, much less talking. Her chest burned.

She wiped tears from her cheeks. Too many broken promises for one lifetime. Too many times someone she'd loved just left her. She turned the shell over in her hand.

"Probably shouldn't have kept this reminder of one more promise that wasn't important."

Adrienne grabbed her hand just before she whipped the shell into the water. "Mom, you have a lot more life to live, a lot more time for new promises. Maybe even for the fulfillment of this one. Don't throw your promise shell away yet." She took the shell from Kendra's hand and nestled it back into the box.

"That was a sweet story. But I feel like you left something out. When you told us you spent the weekend alone with Tommy, there was something in your voice, something that shocked and intrigued us. What did you leave out?"

Kendra winked. "I haven't told you everything about the weekend. Some things shall remain private. I'll give you this much. Remember, I was almost eighteen, he was nineteen, and he was going away. We spent the whole weekend either on the beach or in my house in front of the fireplace. It was romantic and idyllic. It was perfect."

She looked across the marsh. "While I had a measure of faith in those days, I also had my own ideas and values. Right or wrong, they were mine. We should have waited, but as scandalous as it was, it was a beautiful time in my life."

"I predict you'll be able to pick up where you left off." Adrienne grinned.

"Not that way. Now I am a firm believer that true love waits." She stood. "Let's go home. I have a turtle nest to watch *tonight and* I'd like to get a couple hours of sleep before heading out."

CHAPTER ELEVEN

RECONCILIATION

Turtle Night at Mimosa Beach
Present

endra was the first to arrive, just like she and Pa always were. The retreating tide lengthened the beach. Those poor little turtles would have a long crawl if they waited too long. She sat in her chair at the edge of the surf, facing the nest on the beach. The flashlight sat on the ground in front of her.

Pa's patrol light. It would illuminate anything within a fifty-foot radius. Who would believe a big old flashlight could make her feel his presence on the beach? She grinned. He would understand.

Turtle nights had been special for them. He'd sit beside her, holding her hand and sharing his wisdom. Now she sat on the beach in *his* chair with *his* light and an empty hand.

She stared up at the Milky Way.

"I wish you were here to help me, Pa. The past few weeks with the girls have felt like a long year. It's hard sharing this stuff. Heck, it's hard digging it out." She drew circles in the sand with her toes.

"The rest of the items in the box lead to the real tough parts of my life. If only you could help me with this the way you helped me with everything else, even Mother." She wiped her eyes with her hoodie sleeve. "I'm on my own now."

The swishing of sand off bare feet startled her. She wasn't alone. "Best if I stop talking to the sky." Then she recognized the laughter.

"I always knew Mom would crack on her proverbial turtle nights. She's out here at the ocean but not looking at it. Instead, she's facing a sand dune and talking to the stars." Adrienne nudged Arielle. "It's good we got here before anyone else."

Kendra slammed her memory door shut and pasted on a smile. "Mother always said I was a different sort. I always feel close to Pa when I'm out here, so I was talking to him."

"We miss him too, Momma." Arielle sat on the sand beside her while Adrienne kept standing.

"I know you do." She took a cleansing breath. "We always came early to the nest so we could talk. Something about being here in the dark with the ocean behind made it easier to talk about those things we would have avoided otherwise."

"Why?"

"Because the ocean was his happy place. Turtle watching his favorite thing. So, out here he was relaxed and peaceful..."

Kendra chuckled.

"Most of the time that is. I was just now remembering the night he convinced me Mother wasn't like a turtle deserting her young and I needed to forgive her."

Adrienne joined Arielle on the sand. "How did he do that?"

"We were watching a nest." Kendra patted her stomach. "I was about to pop with the two of you. Pa teased me about pulling me in a wagon to the next nest if the babes didn't come soon.

"Stan was on one of his extended business trips. I wasn't due for two months, but he insisted I come here so I wouldn't be alone

84

if you arrived early. I had no problem agreeing to spend a couple of weeks at the beach."

She opened the thermos Adrienne brought and poured some hot chocolate into one of the cups. Then she offered some to them too. They shook their heads.

"Mother came back to Pa after we returned from Europe. He welcomed her with open arms. Somehow I knew she'd stay. And I wasn't happy about it. That was another reason I went to New York after I found out about Tommy and Samantha. I couldn't deal with her invasion into my life with Pa."

Arielle nodded. "Makes sense."

"Yes, but it was wrong. I didn't have a big, fancy wedding because I didn't want my mother there. Pa missed my wedding because he wouldn't come without her. I had a deep, bitter root growing inside me. And two years later Pa wasn't about to let me become a mother who hated her own mom.

"He sat here that night and gave me the lecture of a lifetime... one I didn't want, but sorely needed." Sorely needed? Maybe it was more like long overdue to a spoiled rotten brat. How angry she'd been he chose that night and that subject was when he finally had enough of her tantrum and grudges.

Kendra smiled. "He grabbed my hand and held it tight. I think he knew I would try to get up and leave when he started talking." She laughed. "Like I said, he was a wise man because I did try to pull my hand free when the lecture began. That man had quite the grip.

"He said, 'Kendra Lynn Michaels, you have to let this hate go and forgive your mother. I never been much of a church man, but I do know God and I know you can't live a good life and be a good mother to those two babies if you're busy growing a root of bitterness in your heart. There's not enough room in that little heart of yours to hate and love at the same time.'

"He squeezed my hand and said, 'What Marie did to you was inexcusable. I was furious with her. I know you hurt; I watched it near kill you. I don't begin to know what made her do such a thing. But I do know she regrets it.'"

Kendra brushed her hair from her face. "I got mad at him—no, I was fuming. I yanked my hand from his and stood. I paced. I kicked sand. And ranted—boy, did I rant. Pa just sat there and let me. I don't remember what I said, but it was about the worst case of verbal venting ever. I'm not sure you two have experienced that amount of anger from me. You almost did when you lied about skipping school—"

"What?" Adrienne sat straight up, then slouched. "You knew?"

Kendra nodded. "I was ready to spit bullets. Called your father and let him have it. Told him if he wasn't such a good liar, maybe his daughters wouldn't be either. Oh my, what a fight we had. By the time you got home, I had it out of my system and didn't have the energy to confront you. Besides, you convicted yourselves. I've never seen you two work so hard assuaging your guilt. The entire house got cleaned without my asking."

She grinned.

Arielle nudged her sister. "Told you she knew."

"You didn't hide as many things from me as you thought, but I digress. When I finished my tirade, Pa patted the chair, and I sat back down. He grabbed my hand again. Then, calmly he said, 'Feel better now? If you don't see your way to forgive your mother, you will carry that venom into motherhood and rob those two babies of the beautiful person you are. And that's all I will ever speak about this. The rest is between you and God. And Marie.'"

Kendra watched a line of flashlights approach from the highway. The turtle watchers were coming. It would soon be time to step into the surf and guide the little ones to sea.

"I always thought forgiveness was a once and done kind of thing. And maybe sometimes it is. But for the deep wounds, the ones that ruin lives, it comes in quietly like high tide in the bay. Slowly the water level rises—no waves, no force, just a slow creep.

Before you know it, the basin is filled back up. Once I opened my heart to it, forgiveness filled the bitter places."

Arielle rested her head on Kendra's leg. "How did you do it? And I mean emotionally and literally."

"By that time in my life, I was reading my Bible daily and going to church almost every week. My faith was week, but growing. So, I read every scripture I found about forgiveness, and I kept thinking how Jesus forgave His killers from the cross. The day we brought you two home from the hospital I called Mother and apologized for shutting her out of my life, told her I forgave her, and asked her to come meet her granddaughters."

Kendra rubbed the tops of their heads.

"Mother got on the first plane she could and flew overnight from California to get here. She stayed three days. Forgiving her didn't change the past, but it changed our present and the future. It freed me to rebuild something with her and give you two the chance to have a grandmother.

"The night she left, as I rocked my new babies in my arms, I realized that in a way only He could do, God had blessed my heart through both my mother's control and hardness. Her control made me rebel, but it made me grow up and go out on my own. Without that time in my life I wouldn't have been sitting there holding my daughters. And the hardness she wore like a cloak only covered insecurities. Empathy for the loneliness she had created for herself became bigger than my anger until it faded away entirely."

She picked up the flashlight and blinked it so everyone could find them. The girls turned theirs on too.

"Years later, when Mother was sick, nearing her end, she asked me to take her to the pier. We sat there late afternoon and watched the dolphins. She held my hand in her frail one. Speaking was difficult for her, but it was obvious she had something to say. I leaned close, and she apologized. Even though I had forgiven her years before, it warmed my heart to hear the words. I told her she was forgiven. I think she was waiting to hear those words because she died the next day."

Arielle and Adrienne sandwiched her in a hug.

From a few feet away someone called, "They're coming! Shine those lights this way."

A familiar thrill ran up her spine. No matter how many times she stood in the surf and held light that would attract the turtles to the shoreline and not the highway, she always got choked up watching them scramble toward the ocean, their life journey begun.

Arielle touched her shoulder. "Momma?"

"Yes?"

"Papa was your flashlight on the shore, showing you where to go."

CHAPTER TWELVE

THE PHOTO

*K*endra put the last few items in the canvas tote and hustled it to the Jeep. The first time she'd done this, the girls were six. Running through the house, she'd yelled, "Wake up. It's time for an adventure."

Something about her excitement had made it way more than a picnic. The girls liked it so much, that weekly adventures were a summertime staple until high school. Then it sort of naturally dwindled away.

Kendra glanced at the photo of Tommy and her on the boat before sliding it into her shirt pocket. The girls were right. He was *hot*.

Rushing back inside, she took the stairs two at a time. At their room, she knocked but didn't give them a chance to respond before she rushed inside.

"Hey, you two lazy bones, don't you know what today is?"

Mumbles greeted her.

Not to be deterred, she crossed the room and whipped the drapes open. Sunlight poured in. More mumbles erupted, followed by covers lifting over their faces.

"Wake up. It's time for our adventure."

Adrienne sat up and gave her a curious look. "Aren't we a bit old for that?"

"You're never too old. There's a place I want to show you. I'm pretty sure you've not been there or you would have told me all about it. But we have to be on the tidal schedule today. Meet me at the car. I've got granola bars and coffee for, plus sandwiches and snacks for lunch."

By the time Kendra reached the bottom of the stairs, she heard them moving around and discussing her sanity. She got into the Jeep and waited for them. Her foot thumped the floorboard with the same rhythm her heart pounded. This was going to be so much fun.

Adrienne whooshed into the front seat and puffed her breath out. "This better be good. I didn't even have time for a shower, Mom."

"You won't need one."

Arielle got into the back seat while tying her hair up in a messy bun.

"Okay, let's go."

Kendra backed the car out and headed up the island.

"Mom, we're going to the pier. What's so adventurous about that? We've been here hundreds of times. Should have stayed in bed."

Kendra ignored the complaints and turned into Bayside Marina. Joe Martin met her as she parked.

"Oh my goodness, it's been a while, Mrs. Michaels. That is what I should call you right? We were all just so sorry to hear about your husband. I do hope you are getting along well. I made sure everything is ready just as Mr. Michaels—well I guess you too—wanted. I hope she's the right color and you find her decked out okay. I even had Stephen give her an extra polish job yesterday."

"Thank you, Joe. That was kind of you."

"Nothing's too much for you and your daughters, Mrs. Michaels."

Kendra opened the hatch and got the tote bags. Joe quickly took them.

"Ma'am, you must let me carry these." He started towards the docks. "It's right this way. I made sure to use the slip you always used. I hope that was okay. Oh my goodness, maybe it wasn't. I can change things if you wish."

Kendra's heart knotted. Had Stanton been so demanding the poor man felt like he had to bend over backward for her? "I'm sure everything is fine, Joe. Come on girls. The tide is coming in."

The slip where her father always kept his boat, then Stan kept his, now held hers. She let the girls pass her and watched them freeze when they saw the brand new 23' Monterey Bowrider in the slip. The name painted on the back was *Kendrielle*.

She swallowed the lump in her throat. "This was his surprise to all three of us in honor of your graduation. He told me about it the week before his accident and made me swear you wouldn't know until we brought you here the first time. So, here we are."

Her heart hitched. Stan was a conundrum. He really had been excited about the boat and giving it to his girls. He often did things like that, and she knew they came from his heart. Her husband was like a male version of Hosea's wife. And, she, like Hosea always took her spouse back.

She cleared her throat. No. Not today. This was a happy day and she was about to enjoy the last gift Stan had given any of them, one he'd given to all of them. Today was about good things.

The girls were walking up and down the slip looking at the boat.

Arielle traced her fingers along the stripes on the bow. "It's beautiful."

"Mom, we get to keep it, right?" Adrienne leaned over the edge and read the name. "Who thought of that name? I love it, it could be a real name."

"Everything about this boat was his idea. I knew nothing about it until it was already here in the slip waiting for us. Come on, time's wasting."

She steered the boat across the expanse of what everyone called "Sound Lake. Along the mainland coast was a huge tower. Diving docks poked out from the sides and top, and a water slide wrapped around the tower.

Adrienne gasped. "A water park in the water?"

Kendra nodded. She stopped the boat beside a green park buoy, dropped anchor, then tied the boat to it.

"Mom, this is amazing. Who would ever think to make such a neat place? And why haven't we seen it yet?"

"Because we never come to this end of the island, silly." Arielle nudged Adrienne's shoulder. "I think I know who owns it. Look at the sign."

"TLK WATER FUN?"

They looked at Kendra.

"Mom?"

"Momma?"

"Tommy owns this park."

"He named it after you? That was pretty bold." Adrienne frowned.

Kendra chuckled. "That would have been bold and unwise. You mustn't forget his initials are TLK."

"So, you're saying there is no double entendre?"

"I don't know what he intended. I just know this became his project after Samantha's death. It took him years to get all the environmental approvals and permits. Last summer was his first season, and from what I understand, it is highly successful. The diving tower is only open when the tide is in, but the slides are always open. He built some pretty incredible automatic extenders for the slides when the tide is out."

Kendra pointed to red flags at the base and top of the diving tower. "When those flags switch to green, the tide is in and diving is open. I figure they will open in about thirty minutes. Your suits are in your bags. Go ahead and change, then we can eat some granola while we wait."

Kendra wasn't sure she could eat. Her stomach had knotted into a macramé ball when she dropped anchor. Maybe Tommy wasn't at work today and her anxiety was for naught. How could she look into his eyes and not fall apart? Yet, every part of her longed to look into them, search them, and maybe finally know how he felt. There, she said it. Or thought it, anyway.

Arielle finished her granola bar, brushed the crumbs from her hands and reached into the tote for her swimsuit. "I'm impressed." She stared at the expanse and shook her head. "Can't help but wonder how a farmer turned beach bum came up with such an ingenious idea."

Kendra removed the photo from her pocket. "He had some help."

🐢

Anchored in Sound Lake
July 4, 1989

Tommy and I climbed back into the boat after a long swim and spread our towels on the bow. He lay down, and I snuggled into the crook of his arms. Between the water and sunshine on my skin and the nearness of him, I was about crazy with tingles. He kissed the top of my head then stared at the sky.

"Kenna, I can't believe you won't be going to State with me. It's not fair. All these years I've been telling you to cut your mom some slack, and now she's taking you from me. Don't think she likes me."

He was right, so I lied. "It's not that she doesn't like you. She's just a snob and wants me to be one too."

I snuggled tighter in his embrace. "But I love you and Pa loves you and that's all that matters."

"Know what I want to do some day?"

"Marry me."

"Nope."

I sat up and glared at him. "You don't want to marry me?"

"Don't be silly. That's a given. I will marry you. I'm talking about something else."

"So, what is it?"

"I don't know really. Well, let me start again."

He sat up and pulled me close again.

"I love this lake and swimming here and diving off the boat. The other day I saw a boat with a little pool slide on it. The kids would slide into the water. They were having a blast."

"I saw that too. I thought if I had seen that when I was little, I would have bugged Pa until he got me one."

He nodded. "And he would have."

"Probably."

"That slide got me to thinking. What if somebody built a water slide over there along the coast, where the lake is deepest and even deeper at high tide?"

"Ooh, I like that. What if it had a tower with diving boards and all?"

He shook his head. "Not deep enough when the tide is out."

"True. Would it be deep enough at high tide?"

"Yeah, I think so."

We sat on the bench and stared at the shore, both lost in our own imaginations. Flying off a high dive into crystal blue water filled my mind. We stayed there a while, just sitting in silence—something we often did. In moments like this, we shared as much as when we talked.

"There'd be lots of crazy permissions, applications, fees, and who knows what else I'd have to get."

"Not to mention it would cost a small fortune to build it." I leaned on his shoulder and melted into him. "What would you call it?"

He tilted my chin up and kissed me.

"TLK Water Fun."

"Little proud to name it after yourself, don't you think?" I teased.

He tickled my ribs then kissed me again. Deeper. Better. The kind of kiss that turned me to mush. "Not my initials, turtle girl. Named after the girl I love. So don't get me mad at you, or I'll change my mind. Shall we go over there and daydream a bit?"

"Sure." I would go anywhere with him, daydreams or not.

We tied the boat to the old pier at the edge of the river and sat on the boards. He pointed to the shore.

"The tower have to jut into the water a bit, and I'd put one- and three- meter diving boards. Maybe even a seven-meter diving dock if the water is deep enough." He nudged me. "I know you'd probably be the only person who'd dare dive off the seven-meter one, much less anything higher. But I'd put it there just for you.

"Then there would be twin water slides that start over land and wrap around the dive tower and dump people into the lake."

"What about when the tide goes out and the water is too shallow? You can't have some kid land too hard on the bottom."

"True. I'll have to think on that."

"What about extensions?"

"Huh?"

"You know. When the tide is in, the slide ends higher. When it is out, the extensions make it longer so they are still dumped into a pool of sorts?"

"I like that."

Happy silence again.

"What about a swimming pool?"

"In the lake? That's a little extreme don't you think?"

I punched his arm. "Now who's being silly? I mean on land. A pool for people who don't want to slide or dive. Maybe even a kid's mini-park. That way, when the tide is out, there's still stuff to do."

"I like it. See? I knew I kept you around for a reason."

"When will you build this?"

"I guess after I get independently wealthy."

We sat a while, then swam, then sat some more.

An old man with an armful of fishing poles worked his way to the end of the pier. He nodded at us as he set his poles up. "You kids have a good day?"

"The best." Tommy stood then reached down to help me up. "Time for us to go though. Could you maybe take a picture of us on the boat, sir?"

"Be happy to."

After helping me into the boat, Tommy passed the camera to the old man.

TLK WATER FUN
Present

Kendra stared at the photo in her hand. "And here it is. That was the best day."

"Sounds to me like pretty much every day with Tommy was the best day." Adrienne elbowed her sister. "You said the park wasn't named after you."

"No, I said TLK are his initials. Prior to this summer, I hadn't seen him since Pa died, so how would I know?"

"Sometimes you can't see what's in front of you."

"Excuse me?"

"It's a message. He named the park exactly what he told you he would. He's sending you a message to say he remembers."

Arielle perked up. "Yeah, that's it. How romantic."

"Well, you two have always been hopeless romantics. This is my first time here too."

Adrienne stood. "So, you haven't tried those diving boards yet?"

Kendra shook her head. "Thought we might do it together."

"And maybe you'll see Tommy."

"I am forty-seven years old, not some lovesick teenager. If he's here, we'll surely see him. He'll remember you even if you don't him. Just don't embarrass me."

They spoke together. "Us embarrass you? Never."

Oh dear. She clapped her hands together. "The flag just went green."

"How do we get there?"

Kendra pointed to a boat speeding in their direction. "Attaching to the buoy signaled them. It's on the way to get us."

Kendra was next in line on the seven -meter platform. Any minute, she'd experience the moment of zero gravity before the descent. She walked to the end and looked down. It was a bit different to be looking at bay water instead of a clear blue pool. She backed up, set her stance, approached and then dove.

Adrienne and Arielle raced up the steps after her. Kendra lost count of how many times they'd run up the steps and leaped into the water. But by the time they had also raced each other up the slide, her legs screamed at her to stop the marathon. She couldn't keep up with them. Thankfully the tide would give her a respite.

"I lost track of the time, but I figure the yellow flag will be up soon. How about one more and then we'll eat our picnic on the boat?"

Adrienne jumped up. "You're on!"

Kendra stood on the upper dock, looking around at the expanse of the park. "You really did it, Tommy." Everything they daydreamed about years ago was right here, for real. She was so proud of him.

"Next," the lifeguard called.

She approached the edge, raised her arms, arched her back and floated into a swan dive. The moment of suspension, weightlessness was like floating through the air. Then she closed her arms into position and stretched into the water.

As she propelled to the surface and popped her head out of the water, she heard Adrienne and Arielle cheering. The dive felt great, but she knew her form suffered from lack of practice. The two of them really didn't know how bad it was.

"Mom, that was great." Adrienne stood by the ladder.

Arielle was on the other side. "I have never seen you dive prettier than that. Was it frightening?"

Before Kendra could respond, both girls straightened up and backed away from the ladder. Kendra reached for the rails and got her feet on the bottom rung before she looked up. A hand reached for hers.

"I saw the dive and knew. No one but Kendra Michaels would brave that height and do such a beautiful swan dive."

Tommy. Her feet slipped off the ladder, and she slid under the water. Oh dear. Maybe she could just swim away, but she hadn't taken a deep breath. Surfacing was necessary.

She grabbed the ladder and quickly pulled herself up and out of the water. Standing face to bare-tanned-ripped chest, she swallowed then looked up.

"H-hey, Tommy."

"Kenna."

The softness in his voice wrapped around her heart like the towel he offered caressed her shoulders. Had it been years or only minutes since she was last in his arms? Time did a funny thing when their eyes locked.

After seconds or days—which was it?—he cleared his throat and looked at the dock. "It's good to see you again."

The pregnant silence was about to give birth to words and feelings she'd held at bay for many years. The emotion was bigger than she could handle.

Tommy smiled at her. "Don't turtle up on me, Kenna. All those things can be said in their own time." He turned toward the girls. "I'm Tommy King. Haven't seen either of you since you were little. Let me see, Arielle was the long-haired one. Still?"

They nodded.

Kendra struggled to keep from bursting into laughter at her blubbering girls. It shouldn't be legal for a middle-aged man to look that good.

Tommy shook their hands and then faced her again. Chocolate pools begged her to dive in. She stared at her feet.

"Would you like to join me for supper?"

Yes. She shook her head. "We can't. The tide will start out soon, and I can't have our new boat get beached. When the yellow flag comes up, we have to head out."

"Okay. How is Arthur?"

"He's a darling. I love him. Thank you."

"Welcome. Seriously, come anytime. There's no charge for my loved ones."

Loved ones?

"Umm…thank you." She stared at the water, wouldn't look in his eyes again lest she fall in. "But we do have to go. There's the yellow flag."

They hesitated then followed.

Adrienne stopped at the end of the pier. "Mom. What's wrong with you? We don't have any plans. The little transport dingy isn't here yet. We could have stayed longer."

Kendra couldn't begin to explain what being in his presence did to her or know how to deal with the resurfacing feelings. It was better to avoid expressing them, than to risk finding out he didn't feel the same.

"He didn't really mean it. He was just being neighborly."

"Since when is calling someone 'a loved one' being neighborly?"

Arielle laughed so loud people around them stared. "Wow, you really are out of the loop. Didn't you see his face? He couldn't take his eyes off you."

"Yeah, right."

"Didn't he, Adrienne?"

She nodded. "Absolutely. We really should stay."

Kendra crossed her arms and stepped onto the dingy. "It's time to go."

The twins trudged to the boat and plopped on the bench beside her. Once they got on the *Kendrielle* she busied herself getting ready to leave. Why did he have to look so good? Why hadn't he followed them?

"Momma?"

"Yes?"

"He's watching us."

Sure enough, he stood at the very end of the pier watching them leave. Unable to deal with the carousel of emotions, she grabbed the photo from the console and shoved it into her pocket.

"Mom?"

She turned toward Adrienne.

"He's *still* hot."

CHAPTER THIRTEEN

THE STARFISH RING

Mimosa Beach, NC
Present

A full moon, low tide and a distant coastal storm provided a crazy surf. Between waves knocking her down, sand filling her suit, and the blasted riptide doing its best to suck her out to sea, Kendra gave up on any ocean therapy. She dragged herself into the breakers as one more wave took her feet out from under her.

Perfect. The ocean had mimicked her emotions all morning. She plopped on her towel and watched the clouds. After lunchtime, the Fourth of July Regatta would begin. Mimosa Beach would become one big celebration.

She suffered from what Pa used to call spaghetti brain. One moment she'd be happy about celebrating the girl's twenty-third birthday today and then she'd tear up and realize she actually missed Stan. Which was itself a rather new and okay emotion. Before she had a chance to embrace the feeling, she'd see that woman standing by the trees at the funeral. Crying.

Kendra shook her head. Sirens in the distance made her think of police investigation. What impact would TJ's trial have on them? Arthur barked at a sand crab. And always there was Tommy.

She turned the ring on her middle finger in circles, touching each starfish etched into the gold around the band. It was the one memento she never put into the box. It was also the one falsehood she'd perpetuated. Everyone assumed she'd bought it for herself. It had not come off her finger since the night Tommy put it on. That summer came back to her with a flood of emotions...

July 3, 2005
One day before Arielle and Adrienne's 10th Birthday

"I have to go to New Bern for an all-day meeting tomorrow."

"On the Fourth of July?"

"Yes, it's a cookout meeting. I'll get to your father's house before the girls go to bed."

"After all of these years, you still don't call him Pa or Dad. Why, Stan?"

"I have a father; he's yours." He finished his coffee and set the mug on the counter. "What time does the party start?"

Way to change the subject. I'd told him the plans at least a hundred times. The presents I'd just wrapped lay on the kitchen table.

"I thought we were going to make the whole day a party for them. There goes that idea."

"Don't start with me, Kendra."

"Don't you want to be there when they get that new Sunfish?"

"They're only ten. The next day the three of us can go sailing in Sound Lake all day. One day won't make a difference."

"Sure it will. But I'll ask Pa to take them to the regatta while I get ready for the cookout. Think you can tear away from her and be here in time for the fireworks?"

"Of course I c—" He glared at me. "What's that supposed to mean. I said I'll be in a meeting all day."

"Sure you will."

"*Woman.* Push, you always push. A man never gets any peace. If you don't believe me why not come and check on me?"

He slammed the door so hard our wedding photo fell off the wall. I left the shattered pieces on the floor and stormed upstairs.

The next day, after the girls finished breakfast and Pa took them to the park, I drove to New Bern. If there was an all day meeting it wasn't at the office. The place was locked up tight. I let myself in and walked the dark hall to Stan's office suite.

He wasn't in a meeting. And he wasn't working. Nor was he alone. His newest secretary sat on his desk, facing him, wearing his shirt. She had the gall to laugh at me as I came in.

I walked to the desk and soundly slapped him.

"You, Stanton Michaels, are a scoundrel. A weekend with this secretary is more important than your daughters' tenth birthday."

I glared at the buxom blond and poked her shoulder. "You are only one in a long line of conquests. He will not leave me and marry you. You will not get any of his money. And no matter how many promises he's made you, he won't be any more faithful to you than he is to me. I see the arrogant disbelief in your eyes. It doesn't matter to me whether you believe me or not. I know my husband."

I stormed out, slowing only long enough to rake everything off of the secretary's desk and dump her precious scarlet cyclamen all over the floor.

As he raced into the hallway in his skivvies and T-shirt, I heard her swearing behind him.

The elevator chose that moment to be slow. Stan pulled me into his arms.

"I'm sorry, honey. You're right. I am a scoundrel and. I don't deserve you or the girls or anything."

"No, you don't." I pulled free of his embrace. "Go away. I can't stand the sight of you. Don't touch me. For heaven's sake, she's wearing your shirt. Go back in there and do whatever. I don't care anymore. Nothing matters except Adrienne and Arielle. If you decide to come, call first. I don't want to see you. I'm taking the rest of the summer to figure out what to do."

"About what?"

"You."

"You wouldn't divorce me."

"Why not?"

"Because you promised."

"You made that same promise. How's it working for you?"

"Kendra, you know they don't mean anything to me."

"And that should make me feel better?" I pressed the elevator button. "I'll tell the girls you're working on their birthday. The new boat will make up for your absence. Not."

Thankfully, he hesitated instead of following me into the elevator. The doors closed before he could step inside. I left the lobby and ran to my car. Stan raced out the door as I backed out of the parking space. To anyone watching he was a remorseful husband. If only they knew. Since status and standing in the community were all important, that's what he wanted them to see.

I sped away and didn't slow down until I crossed the causeway bridge onto Mimosa Beach Island. Too bad I couldn't draw the bridge up and keep Stan away.

After calling Pa and giving him the CliffsNotes version, I drove to the end of the island. The turtle station would be quiet. I removed my shoes and socks, rolled up my jeans, and twisted my hair into a sloppy bun.

When I stepped onto the beach, my toes sank into the cool sand. Ahh. "When hard pressed I cried to the Lord and he brought me to a spacious place." That verse from Psalm118 was my comfort. Coming to the turtle shack and this part of the island was always my spacious place. I took one of the old chairs leaning against the turtle shack to the water's edge, sat down and stretched my feet into the water.

At first it was a tear here and there. Then more. When the deluge hit, my shoulders shook until I was trembling. I hyperventilated. Couldn't stop. Actually didn't try.

A breaker came in high and fast and drenched me. The salt of tears mingled with the ocean spray. And I realized I wasn't alone.

Don't know if I sensed him or detected his cologne first. But I looked around and saw Tommy sitting in the sand several feet behind my chair. He said nothing, didn't move, just winked.

I faced the water again. "How long have you been here?"

"Long enough."

Comfortable silence stretched. He remained behind me. I kept watching the water.

"How'd you know I was here?"

His soft voice caressed my ears. "I was visiting your pa when you called. Knew this was where you'd come."

"I could always count on you."

"Not always, Kenna."

"True."

He walked up behind me and placed his hands on my shoulders. Then he kissed the top of my head. A whispered "I love you" drifted past my ear, or was that just a whoosh of ocean breeze?

"Kenna, I'm sorry."

"For what?"

"Everything."

I was too. "Yeah."

"What will you do?"

"Don't know."

We stayed on the beach until sunset. Not talking, just being. I had more peace in those few hours than I'd had for years.

That summer we spent many hours walking and talking. Stan

came to visit when I agreed he could. Pa was my rock. I don't know how many times I told Tommy I would leave Stan so we could be together. He refused each time, telling me I'd regret it.

Accepting reality, I loaded the car to go home. Tommy stood quietly by and after closing the trunk I turned around into his embrace. He pulled away and took something from his pocket.

"Kenna, I know you love turtles and sand dollars, but the starfish is my favorite. When life beats it up and breaks it, the starfish grows new points to replace the broken ones. I pray the breaks in your heart will grow into new joy for you."

Tears streamed down my cheeks.

"Don't cry. I do believe our day will come. But this is not it."

And I went back to regular life. Stan behaved for a while. And everyone thought I bought the ring for myself.

Mimosa Beach
Present

Kendra filled the sink with dishwater. Arielle and Adrienne brought dishes in.

"What did you two do all day?"

"We watched the regatta, then went to the water park. You should've come. It was crowded, but it was a blast." Arielle was drying the dishes then handing them to Adrienne to put away. "Where were you?"

"I was on the beach. Waves were rough, but the sunshine was nice."

"We thought you would join us."

"It's okay for you to do things just you. I was fine."

"Momma, this island isn't big enough for you to avoid him forever. We spent the day at the park and only saw him a few times. He was busy."

Adrienne nudged Kendra. "But, I'm real sure he kept looking for you. Why were you hiding at the beach?"

"I wasn't. Just didn't want to see him and ruin your day."

"How exactly would seeing him ruin our day?" Arielle dried the last dish and draped the towel on the sink. She turned to face Kendra. "I don't understand what's holding you back. You're both single and obviously still in love—"

Kendra twirled toward her daughters. The plate she was putting away slipped from her grip and crashed to the floor.

"We. Both. What?"

"Aw, come on. Adrienne and I watch the way your eyes light up when you tell us the stories. Funny thing, when we go to the park, his eyes do the same thing when he asks us how you're doing."

Adrienne handed the broom and dustpan to Kendra, an amused look on her face. "Stop twirling that ring long enough to clean up your mess, Mom. I'm not walking across the floor in my bare feet."

The girls talked to Tommy about her?

She swept up the shards of plate in short order. Kendra shoved the broom into the corner and faced them.

"I'm not avoiding or hiding. I'm processing. Are you joining me for the fireworks?"

"Wouldn't miss them." They spoke together.

Kendra opened the door to let Arthur out. Following him down the steps, she crossed the yard and walked to the pier. She wasn't avoiding him. Really. After all, hadn't she taken them to the water park the first time? Hadn't she kept Arthur? Tommy knew where she lived, where she walked every day. If he was still in love with her he could certainly find her. Of course, he had put the ball in her court years ago. But that was beside the point.

When the girls joined her, she helped them spread the quilt on the dock. All three of them lay back and watched the sky. The fireworks display wouldn't start until after dusk. They had a good thirty minutes to count the stars as they came out. When there were more stars than they could count, they silently enjoyed the island sounds. The mosquito buzzing around her ear wasn't even annoying her.

The first fireworks shot into the night sky, their illumination blocking the stars. A brilliant golden starburst exploded then rained glittering embers into the bay. Their oohs and ahs joined with those of others all around the neighborhood. Kendra had spent most of her Fourth of Julys at this very spot, doing this very thing. Something felt right and perfect about it. No stress, no turmoil, no need to fret about anything.

The next starburst lit the sky, turning everything pink and making them glow. Blast after blast rained sparkles and color on them and the entire bay. It was one of the best displays they'd ever had.

"Momma?"

"Yes, Arielle?"

"You didn't buy that starfish ring for yourself, did you?"

Why'd she have to bring that up? She didn't answer.

Adrienne reached over and grasped her hand. "Your silence yells at us. That's probably one of the few lies you've ever told."

Kendra's tongue stuck to the roof of her mouth. Before she could answer, the grand finale burst across the sky like a rainbow of shooting stars.

They remained on the pier long after the smoke cleared and the crowds had gone.

"It was the only time I ever lied to you all. I apologize."

Silence hung in the air like the smell of sulfur that had dissipated with the smoke.

Kendra sat up and stared over the dark water. Silence between them had never felt ominous before. She searched for words but found none. The only way to bridge this was to share this part of the story too.

Before she could start, Arielle sat up.

"Adrienne, it's time. We're asking her to share important things. We should too. No more secrets."

"You're right."

Kendra frowned.

"Momma, we need to tell you about graduation weekend."

CHAPTER FOURTEEN

CAUGHT

*A*rielle twisted her hair into a bun and stared across the black water. Her shoulders heaved in a great sigh. "But first, can I ask you something?"

"Anything."

"When did you first learn dad had cheated on you?"

"The first time, just after our first anniversary."

"You could have left him."

"I was young. Afraid. Insecure. Then I got pregnant with you two. I wasn't strong enough to leave him and be a single mother." Kendra looked at Arthur curled up in her lap.

"Year after year, you stayed. Why?"

Kendra couldn't look up. Couldn't speak.

Adrienne touched her shoulder. "Mom, please tell us. It's important."

"I was ten when my mother left. Her own needs overrode mine. Tommy left me for his own physical urges. Stan cheated on me for his. I felt like I wasn't worthy of anyone keeping promises to me. You two were the most beautiful blessings in my life and I refused to ever put my happiness before yours. I swore I would not desert you the way everyone in my life except Pa had me. In my mind, a divorce and divided custody meant anytime you were with him and not me was a desertion on my part. So I stayed."

Arielle nodded at Adrienne. "Go ahead and tell her."

"We want to tell you exactly what happened graduation weekend."

"I thought you already did."

"Not all of it. You twirl that starfish ring when you are stressed. It ties in with that weekend. Last night we decided it was time to come clean."

Kendra looked down and realized she was twirling the ring right then. How often did she do that without thought? She stopped and looked at Adrienne.

"We were so excited about graduation weekend. All of our friends were coming, and we planned to take the boat out and water ski and play all weekend. We knew you were outdoing yourself cooking all sorts of goodies and meals, plus getting the house ready for the onslaught.

"Momma, it was funny at first. We got onto the interstate and realized in our rush to leave we had left our suitcases at the front door. Talk about feeling stupid!

"We stopped at McDonald's then headed back home for our bags. When we left, Dad was still home because he had some work to do there before he hit the road. So we pulled into the drive ready for him to really pick on us for being such airheads."

Arielle's shoulders tensed and she wrung her hands. "Another car was parked next to his in the drive. We didn't think much about it, because we figured it was probably someone from work."

Kendra's jaw tightened.

"We pulled up and rushed into the house, laughter at our absentmindednes. He wasn't in the house, but we heard voices from the pool." She looked at her lap. "Adrienne—I can't do this."

Kendra grabbed the hands. "You don't have to. I can figure out the rest from here."

Adrienne shook her head. "No, you can't. Not all of it.

"Neither of us thought much about him being in the pool. Figured he was taking a break before doing his work. We ran out the back door and hollering he wasn't going to believe what we did.

"We found our father... in the pool with his secretary... pretty sure they were naked and well—ugh, it was disgusting. He came to the edge and draped his arms over the side. He was actually grinning. He reached for his towel and managed to wrap himself up as he exited the pool. He tossed her his robe."

Kendra took Arthur off her lap, stood and paced the end of the pier. Of all the arrogance. He took his mistress to their house, to her house, and had the gall to grin about being caught.

"Momma, stop." Arielle reached up for her hand. "Please sit back down."

She did. Taking a deep breath, she shoved her rage deeper. Her daughters needed her to be calm and attentive rather than ready to kill an already dead man.

Adrienne continued. "He wasn't the slightest bit ashamed. His excuse was that he had a lot of stress and sometimes needed to do something for himself. Then right in front of the woman he said the affairs meant nothing to him and you knew about them."

Arielle half-chuckled. "Miss Mason's reaction to Dad implying she meant nothing to him was poetic justice to watch. When we left, he still had a hand print from her slap."

"Mom, it was ugly. Even the ever-calm Arielle lost it. She said things to Dad that had me blushing. I was proud of her. And about half scared to ever make her that mad at me.

"We told him he was not welcome at the beach that weekend, and if he came, we'd tell you what happened. He glared at us and said, ""Like that frightens me. Your mother won't do anything. She knows deep down I love her. Besides, I'm not the only bad guy here. Ask her to tell you the truth about who gave her that starfish ring she wears.""

Arielle stood and punched her fists together. "I told him I

didn't think for a second you'd ever cheated on him. He laughed as he turned back to the pool." She looked across the dark bay.

"I never had an affair."

"We knew that. That's why we never mentioned it. But, Momma, could you tell us about the ring now?"

They were right—no more secrets, not even the ring. Her daughters loved her, and the three of them needed each other. This summer was proving that. So, she relayed the story of the starfish ring to them.

🐢

They sat there long after she finished talking. The tide cycled out. Kendra rubbed her swollen eyes. She was here when the sun set yesterday, and if she went to the beach now, she could watch it rise again.

Arielle stretched. "I'm going to bed." She kissed Kendra's cheek. "I love you, Momma. Can't say I fully understand why you stayed with Dad, but I have always respected you. Still do. I do wish you'd give some serious thought to contacting Tommy. We're big girls now. Maybe for once in your life, think of your own happiness."

Kendra shook her head.

Adrienne chimed in. "People can change, you know? Grams did. What if your happy ever after hasn't begun yet? And maybe, just maybe, if you put yourself first, we will be even happier. It bears thinking about, Mom. Get some sleep."

She watched them go inside.

Sleep? Not likely.

Should she contact Tommy? Was she ready to allow her heart to hope again? If only she could get some sort of sign. Of course, he'd spoken to the girls about her, and they said he was still in love with her. Those could be signs. Or not.

Kendra took Arthur inside and put him in his crate. She

grabbed a sweater and went to the turtle shack. Once inside, she turned on the battery-operated lamp and slipped into her beach sneaks. It was late in the season for nest-building, but she might as well be productive.

Kendra walked to the end of the island where sea met the bay. The water was always agitated there. It was nice to see something that looked more agitated than she felt. As she approached the water's edge she noticed another lone soul about a hundred yards from her. She'd know that posture anywhere.

Pa always said there are no coincidences, only miracles God didn't get credit for. Here she was, on the beach right after wishing for a sign about contacting Tommy and he happened to be there too. After a sleepless night, she wasn't sure she was ready to make this decision yet. Maybe she could quietly slip away.

"Kenna!"

Guess not.

He caught up to her in short order.

"Don't go, please."

"How'd you know I was about to?"

"Everything about you screamed escape."

"I don't know what to say."

"Then say nothing."

He touched her chin and tilted it. "Look up, Kenna."

She knew what that meant. Her eyes locked with his then he lowered his mouth to hers. The kiss was soft and sweet. Too soon he pulled back and smiled down at her. He caressed her cheek and stepped back.

"Welcome home, Kenna."

"You said that weeks ago."

"I know. But that was to welcome you home *to me*. I just wanted you to know I'm glad your back and I've been hoping maybe it's time for 'destemy' and all that."

Then he turned and walked up the beach.

CHAPTER FIFTEEN

THE NOTE

"*A*rthur Michaels, you drop that shoe right now." Kendra threw her hands in the air as the puppy yipped, wagged his tail, then ran underneath the porch with the dress shoe he'd stolen from her closet. She stared at the trail of debris he had scattered across the yard.

Puppies were work. Like she needed more work in her life right now. The little guy was destroying what little order she had restored in her life. She got on hands and knees and peered underneath the porch. Arthur dropped the shoe and ran to her, covering her face with sloppy, stinky, wonderful puppy kisses. She grabbed the shoe then walked onto the porch.

"I don't care how cute you are. All is not forgiven." He kissed her more, his little tail beating a happy rhythm against her stomach.

"Seriously, Arthur, you are in trouble."

Kendra shook her head and chuckled. It was easy to sound tough, but she couldn't stay mad at the squirmy guy. "You'll have to behave better than this on the boat today, little buddy."

Three weeks had passed since the kiss. No word, no sign of Tommy since that night. How should she interpret that? Her brains had turned to spaghetti again. She alternated between desiring to call him or him to call her. Then she'd long to slap him for toying with her heart again. Or she'd hope to see him but immediately never want to again.

They entered the kitchen as the oven timer beeped. She placed the bread on the cooling rack and filled the sink.

"Smells yummy in here, Mom." Adrienne reached over her shoulder and grabbed a cookie and he examined the table top. "What's bothering you Mom?"

"Nothing."

"Liar. Cinnamon raisin sweet bread, blueberry muffins, chocolate chip cookies, and snicker doodles. You've obviously been baking for hours. This much baking is usually directly proportional to your stress level."

"Spoken like a math teacher."

Adrienne held her hands, palm up in front of her. "I am what I am." She brushed the crumbs off her hands, then poured a cup of coffee. "Tell me what's wrong."

"Summer will be over before I know it, and you two will leave. Arthur's been a brat all morning. Tommy kissed me three weeks ago, then disappeared. The contractor is coming next week and wants a project list, which I have not begun yet. And I have to get the house in Richmond ready to sell. To name a few."

Adrienne slammed her mug sloshing hot coffee over her hand. She pulled it away and shook it. "What did you say?"

"I'm not repeating all of that. I caused myself even more anxiety just listing it all."

"I don't want all of it, just one. Tommy kissed you?"

"Umm, did I say that?"

Adrienne nodded.

"I didn't mean to let that out." She turned to the sink and attacked the mixing bowl with the scrubby. "It's no biggie."

Adrienne reached into the water and grabbed her hand. "Sure it's not. Sit down and tell me about it."

"No."

"Mom no more secrets, right? Something tells me you need to get this out. What is it Tommy would say…don't turtle up on me. Just tell me what happened."

Kendra snagged a dish towel and plopped down at the table. As she unfolded and refolded the towel she relayed what happened that early morning after the fireworks.

"Why would he kiss me like that, and then just disappear?"

"He's waiting for you."

"Huh?"

"Look, I'm certainly no expert on relationships. Heck I am not even in one. From what I see, Tommy made the first move by inviting you back into his life. He won't force himself on you but will wait for you to renew the relationship."

"Maybe so. I'm not ready."

Kendra returned to the sink. "I'll finish the dishes. It's almost noon and I've been baking since before sunrise. Go wake your sister already. I want to go to Picnic Island today, but the tide will be against us before long."

"Sure thing." Adrienne kissed her cheek before racing upstairs.

Kendra touched her shirt pocket to make sure the note was safely tucked inside. She placed a container of the cookies she'd baked into the top of the cooler and headed to the Jeep. This would be their last excursion on the Sound Lake before the girls moved into their new house. Summer always went too fast, especially this one. Although she loved fall on the beach, she would miss these days with Arielle and Adrienne.

Arielle rushed out.

"Come on Adrienne. Momma is already out here."

Adrienne joined her sister outside, and they crossed the yard hand in hand.

Kendra smiled at her daughters—twenty-three years old and still like little girls going on one of their adventures.

Morning , Momma."

"It's hardly morning, dear."

Arielle hugged her then winked. "Adrienne told me about the kiss. We'll talk later."

"Maybe. Would one of you grab Arthur? The tide is in. If we get moving, we can anchor at the island before it goes out."

Adrienne got Arthur situated in the car. "I can't believe we haven't been to Picnic Island all summer, but the waterpark took precedence."

Kendra pulled onto the road. "We do have to get there at least once. Ever since Hurricane Agnes created it in '72 I think people return here and heave a collective sigh that it survived another hurricane season."

At the marina, they loaded the boat quickly and got underway. Adrienne took the helm and sped into the lake, steering the boat in happy circles, causing it to bounce over its own wake.

Kendra looked at the wild-eyed puppy and grinned. Thankfully, she had secured his crate and placed him inside. If only he would think this bumpy ride was punishment and decide to never steal her shoes again.

As they neared the island, Adrienne slowed the boat then anchored close to one of the buoys. Arielle tied the line to tie it. Kendra grabbed Arthur, while the girls loaded the small raft which they'd use for floating the basket, cooler, and beach bag in as they waded the rest of the way to shore.

Kendra looked at her watch. "Okay, ladies we have exactly four hours before we have to pack up and get out of here."

"Mom, after all of these years, don't you trust us to figure out when the tide starts going back out so we can leave in time?"

Kendra watched the wispy clouds and chuckled. "You're right. Each of us should be able to tell what the tide is doing and be out of here safely. If we want to."

Once on land, they spread the blanket, set out their picnic and plopped down. Arthur busied himself chasing the water as it lapped the shore.

She reach inside her shirt pocket and retrieved one of the letters. Its folds were creased and fragile. She unfolded it. "Getting stranded on this island can be wonderful and nerve racking at the same time."

They stared at her.

"It depends upon the company you're with. I got this note after the last time I was stranded here."

"Last time, Mom? Just how many times did you miss the tide?"

"A bunch. But I was never alone when I did." She nudged their shoulders. "Those are other stories. Let's stick to this one. This actually happened before the Starfish ring."

Picnic Island
August 18, 2009

I watched the wake from the speedboat slapping the shore. They were probably on their way back to the marina since the tide was on its way out. I should head back too, but my mind buzzed with too many thoughts. Pa knew where I was. He could find me if he needed to.

I opened the note once more and inhaled the faint but lingering scent. It still sent shivers up my spine. I curled my toes into the sand and read.

Kenna,

Arthur told me he would see you get this. I didn't think
Stanton would be happy about you getting a letter from

me. I'm sure you know Samantha passed away last year. She held on as long as she could. In the end I brought her to the island so she could watch the water. She died in her room at Mom and Dad's house.

I am thankful she didn't suffer as long as her mother. Her last days were peaceful. I read to her or carried her to the pier and sat with her. Sometimes I even floated her in the water. As sensitive to touch as she was, the water restored her.

But now she's gone. I sold Mom and Dad's house. Was hard to move, but it was harder staying there with all of the ghosts of years gone by. I moved to the little blue bungalow at the north end of the island. I love the intensity of the ocean waters crashing into the bay. And there was a turtle nest beside my deck this summer.

I don't know what your life is like these days. I'm sure the girls are beautiful like their mother. I hope you are well.

Kenna, the last week of her life, Sam looked at me and told me I had been a good husband to her. She thanked me. Imagine that—thanking me for being a good husband. I didn't know how to respond. Two days later, as the sun set over the bay, she leaned on my shoulder and said, "I'll not be here much longer. Tommy, go to her. It is time."

The next morning she was gone.

It has taken me a year to be ready to write this letter. But, here it is. Kenna, I have always loved you. I was faithful, and Sam knew it. But she also knew my heart was divided. I guess what I am saying is, if the day ever comes you find yourself alone and your heart still holds love for me, all you have to do is send me a postcard. Write MMM on it. I will come.

Love you forever,
Tommy (TLK)

I folded the letter and placed it in my bag. MMM. Our code for Meet Me at the Mimosa. Thinking of how often we had used that and how quickly we each got to that tree brought a smile. I slipped my water shoes back on and trudged to the water's edge. What I should do is throw the letter in the ocean and forget it.

But I couldn't. I would take it back and put it in my turtle box. Stan would arrive tomorrow with the girls. They'd be all excited from shopping for school clothes with Gramma Michaels. And he'd be eager to get all of us back to Richmond and into his perfect little routine.

As I stood at the water, I realized it was too late. My boat was beached, and there was no way to get back home until early in the morning.

Present

Kendra lay back on the blanket, unable to stop a smile from crinkling her lips.

"You got stranded here alone?" Adrienne shuddered.

"Stranded, yes. Alone, no."

Lying on either side of Kendra, the twins rolled to their sides, mischief shining in their eyes. She kept them waiting a little longer.

"Pa knew what had happened when I wasn't home by dark. He called Tommy since he had an ocean kayak and could get to the island."

Arielle sat up. "Are you saying you spent the night all alone on this island with the love of your life?"

Adrienne cocked her head and sideways stared at her.

Kendra crossed her arms over her chest. "Whose story is this anyway?"

They hushed.

"He kayaked across the bay. The moon was full, so I saw him coming. Knew it was him. I had already wrapped one blanket around me and made a bed roll out of the other. Tommy rowed right up onto the shore and ran to me."

She stood up and walked to the water's edge. Twirling the ring on her finger, she stared across the sound.

"We stayed here all night. Talking. We backed up against the dune and he wrapped me in a blanket he brought."

"It was innocent." She kicked the water. "But, it was the most loved I'd felt in a long time."

There it was. She had shared almost all of her treasures with them, bared almost all of the memories, and ripped open some old scars. Shouldn't she start feeling better soon? She touched the other letter in her shirt pocket.

"There's something else." She removed Stan's letter and offered it to them.

"When I got those files from your dad's safe-deposit box, this was on top of the file. I didn't give it to the police because it was personal. I've prayed a lot about it the past few weeks. I think you two should see it.

"He knew for over a year his life was in danger, thus putting us in danger too. That makes me furious. In his own way, I think he was remorseful for his bad behavior. I'll take Arthur for a little walk while you read it."

Arthur raced along in front of her. He chased ripples in the water, picked up shells the tide had brought in, and every now and then leaped into the water and rolled. The tide was starting to recede. They'd have to pack up and leave soon or be stuck here all night.

He grabbed a large conch shell and tried to pick it up. Failing that, he barked at it. His little bark reverberated in the shell, scaring him, and he ran away from it, stopping between her legs.

Kendra picked him up. "Aren't you just the bravest thing ever? It's a shell, Arthur." She examined for creatures. It was empty. How had that thing ended up here in the sound anyway? Those were usually only found on the ocean side.

She took Arthur back to the girls and sat beside them.

"We need to leave soon. The tide is starting out."

Adrienne handed Stan's letter back. "I think you should give this to the police. They may want the information Dad gave you." She nodded at Arielle. "And we both agree there is nothing keeping you and Tommy apart now. Samantha and Daddy told you to go to each other. Tommy told you he would be here—"

"But that was years ago. Things change."

"Some do, but not this. His kiss should have told you that."

Arielle hugged her shoulders. "It's time for you to send that note with MMM on it."

CHAPTER SIXTEEN

BROKEN SAND DOLLAR AND SHATTERED HEART

The Pier at Home
Present

Kendra sat at the edge of the pier, feet dangling in the water. Arthur had chased butterflies and salamanders all morning as they walked the Preserve Trail and was totally pooped. Now he was curled in a tight little ball in her lap.

Staring across the bay, Kendra rotated the ring. Tomorrow the girls would leave. It was an exciting time for them. Not so much for her. Each breath was a labor. Her chest felt knotted like an old chain necklace. Not to mention the trusty old rib pain had returned a few days ago.

She massaged it then wiped her eyes. How long would the rib hurt this time? It started the day her mother left. Pa took her to doctor after doctor, test after test. They called it intercostal neuralgia. The nerves along that rib fired pain signals to her brain with no physical explanation. Finally, a pain specialist told them Kendra's emotional distress over her mother leaving manifested in the rib pain. He said it would slowly go away. The doctor had been right.

But he failed to warn the pain would return each time her heart broke. It lasted a long time after Pa died. And Stan accused her of making it up to get out of being the wife he needed. Jerk. She rubbed the golf ball of pain under the ribs on her right side. Funny, the pain hadn't returned when he died. Today, the day before the girls would move out, it woke her.

Bare feet padded up behind her. Arielle sat down beside her as Adrienne bent and kissed the top of her head.

"You're rubbing your side. Is it bad today?"

She stopped. "I'm okay."

Adrienne sat on her other side. She reached over and rubbed Arthur's head.

"We're not leaving, Mom, just moving. Wilmington is not that far away. You know we'll be here often. And you can come see us anytime."

Kendra nodded. She swallowed the lump in her throat and wiped another tear.

"Please don't cry."

"Tears are good things, Sweetie."

Arielle offered Kendra the folded tissue paper containing another precious memento. "It's time for the story from this one, Momma."

The sand dollar from the saddest day of her life. Kendra pressed on the pain in her side once more. The memory lay heavy on her heart, but the memento rested lightly in her palm. She carefully unfolded the paper and stared at the broken sand dollar and tiny doves from inside the sand dollar.

Her chin quivered. She bit her lower lip.

The Turtle Shack
July 7, 2012

The tide had come in and flooded my chair a while ago. I didn't care. If only it had taken me out with it. What was left? The only man who had stuck by me was gone. My heart was as empty as Pa's bed.

I wiped salt spray from my puffy eyes then stood. I propped the old chair against the shed wall and headed up the coastline but stopped again. Legs as heavy as my heart prevented me from going further. I picked up clumpy handfuls of sand and whipped them into the ocean.

"It's a Forrest Gump moment." The voice I'd loved all my life spoke from a little further up the shore.

I didn't look toward Tommy. Just whipped more sand.

"I brought a blanket." He wrapped it around my shoulders and stood beside me. "Just in the case there aren't enough fistfuls of sand."

I leaned my head back over against his arm and stared at the black sky.

Silence that gave every emotion a voice encircled us. He smelled of summer and sand and everything my life should have been. First one tear, then a few more, then I sobbed. He placed his arms around my shoulders and held me while tears for every heartbreak I'd ever experienced poured out. It was like all the salt water I'd ingested in my years at the beach dripped onto the sand to return to the sea.

When the deluge subsided, Tommy turned me into his embrace, tilted my chin to look up and kissed my forehead. Afterward, he held my head to his chest. His heart pounded against my cheek.

"I'm sorry, Kenna."

"I know. Me too."

I looked up and he touched my chin. I wanted him to kiss me until the ocean stopped beating the shore. But I knew he wouldn't. He was too honorable. For a moment I longed for him to be the Tommy who'd cheated on me when we were young.

I sighed and leaned against him again.

A rogue wave crashed in and surrounded us in tidal wash. The clouds cleared and moonlight cast shadows on the beach. As the wave receded something lay in the sand at water's edge. Tommy bent and picked up a perfect sand dollar.

"Oh, look. How many years have we wanted to find one of these?"

He caught the tear tracing down my cheek and kissed his finger. "One day, Kenna, one day. Maybe this sand dollar is our sign that one day will happen."

I kicked the sand and my gaze followed the coastline. Other than my girls, nothing in my life had ever really given me a one day. Why would it now?

I started walking towards home.

He hooked his windbreaker on his finger and slung it over his shoulder.

"I don't know what I will do without Pa. He kept me grounded. He guided me through the rough times and always gave me and the girls a haven here. Stan says he wants to sell the beach house. Of course, it's mine and he really has no say, but he will make things miserable if I refuse.

"He almost didn't even show up for the funeral. The only reason he did is that Arielle begged him. He said he had no reason to say goodbye to the old man."

Tommy stopped walking and stared at me in disbelief. He kicked a shell then stomped a few feet ahead of me. His shoulders tensed as his left hand closed into a fist. He punched it into his other hand and kept mumbling "lowlife," through clenched teeth.

After heaving a huge sigh, he faced her. "Kenna, your father was my best friend these past few years. He was the kindest, gentlest man I've ever known. I will miss him. And don't you sell that house. One day you will come back here and stay. Until then, at least you have a refuge when you need it."

He grasped my hand and kissed the top of it. I knew that was the only kiss he would give me. And my wrist warmed at his touch.

"Thank you."

"Aw Kenna, nothing to thank." He looked at the moon overhead. "Did you walk all the way here?"

"Yes."

"Let me drive you home. I parked behind the turtle shack."

"The girls are in bed by now, and Stan's probably on his computer."

"I'll take you anyway. Why not put this sand dollar and the last mimosa flower Arthur gave you in your turtle box?"

I looked sideways at him. "How do you know I still have that old box?"

"I know you. Let's get you home."

He held my hand the whole way there. I came close to begging him to take me home with him. But I couldn't do that to my daughters.

The Pier at Home
Present

Arielle leaned her head on Kendra's shoulder. "I remember that night and the yelling when you got home. I thought Dad was out of his mind. I was scared he would hurt you. But I was afraid to get out of bed too."

Adrienne nodded.

Kendra's shoulders dropped. "I had no idea you two were awake. That was a bad night."

"Momma, tell us what happened. Please. We've waited all summer to find out how Dad got the box and how the sand dollar broke. Honestly, I think maybe you broke that night too. Maybe it's time for God to put the broken pieces to get put back together."

"Aw, sweetie, I hope He will. Pretty sure He's the only one Who can. How about some hot chocolate? We started this summer of stories inside with a fire in the fireplace and hot chocolate. Maybe we should end it the same way."

🐢

Adrienne brought the tray of hot chocolate and the last of the snicker doodles into the family room just as Arielle got the fire flaming. They each took a mug and sat on their poufy chairs. Arthur circled the room several times before curling up on a huge pillow in front of the fireplace.

Kendra took a long, slow sip of hot chocolate. The whipped cream tickled her lips as the hot liquid warmed her inside. "Why do so many people reserve this treat for winter? Of course, I am not sure anyone makes it as good as you, dear. You could open Adrienne's Hot Chocolate Shoppe."

"No thanks, I think I'll stick with teaching math to eighth graders."

"Who in their right mind chooses that job?"

"Me." Adrienne set her mug down. "Mom, we have to talk about that night."

Kendra sighed. She'd known all summer this was coming and still wasn't prepared for it.

"Tommy took me home. I made him drop me off out front and leave. I promised I would call him if I needed him. I think we both knew I wouldn't call. You two were in bed, and Stan was in the office. I went to my desk, wrapped the sand dollar in some tissue paper, and put it inside my box. Stan walked in as I put the box away.

'He glared at me and asked if I'd gotten my little rendezvous all out of my system. When I asked him what he meant, he said he saw guilt all over my face and accused me of being on the beach with Tommy. I told him he was the one who had worn guilt like a trophy our entire marriage.

"I wanted to be a turtle that night, wanted a shell to close into. So, I turned toward Pa's study. All I wanted to do was to curl up on Pa's chair and cry. But Stan was in a hateful mood.

"He cleared the room in two strides and blocked the doorway. When I shrugged and tried to walk away from him, he grabbed my arm and jerked me to face him."

Adrienne's quick intake of breath interrupted Kendra.

"The bruise on your arm, the one that was there for weeks, Dad did that?"

Kendra nodded.

"I wish you had left him."

"I do too. But hindsight is always perfect."

She sipped her drink. It was harder than she expected to speak of this dark side of her husband. She sighed.

"Stan squeezed my arm so hard my fingers went numb. He practically spat the words at me, "Go ahead and deny you were with Tommy."

"I said, 'If I denied, it would be a lie, and I am not the one in this marriage who does that. I was on the beach crying about Pa, and Tommy showed up. He walked with me, and we talked about Pa. He found this sand dollar and then brought me home. That's it, Stan. Nothing like what you would have done on the beach with another woman.'

"He released my arm long enough to slap my cheek, then grabbed the box from my hands and stormed away. He stopped at the front door and snarled at me. "I've heard enough of your accusations. Hell, he cheated on you before I ever did. What is it about you that makes men cheat? Did you ever think of that? I've put up with this stupid turtle box far too long. Time to put the past to death 'Kenna.' I'll be back when I see this box and all of the broken pieces of it floating out with the tide.""

"And until the day you two found the box, I thought he had done exactly that."

Kendra covered her face with her hands. No words described the emptiness inside. She never told anyone what Stan had said to her that night. Not Tommy. Pa was gone. Somehow, the impact of speaking Stan's harsh words out loud hit her like a storm flipping a helpless sailboat at sea.

It had been years since she'd had as many panic attacks as she'd recently had. This one came hard and fast. Her hands trembled. She dropped the mug. She couldn't catch her breath. But her heart beat so hard she thought it would jump out of her chest. When the walls closed in, she pushed the coffee table out of the way and tried to stand, to run away, but couldn't move. Escaping the world became her only focus.

Arielle sat in front of her, tilted her chin so they looked eye to eye. "Breathe with me... In...Out...Slower...In...Out."

Kendra followed her daughter's lead. Moment by moment her breathing slowed, heart calmed, and the tremors racking her body subsided. She walked to the kitchen and grabbed a water bottle. She stood at the back door staring across the sound. The distant illumination from Tommy's water park gave the horizon a rainbow glow.

The girls joined her.

"Stan hit a nerve that night. I had always wondered what was wrong with me that made Tommy and then him be unfaithful. I think you're right. Something in me broke that night. Stan got better for a while. I allowed myself to think he'd had a change of heart. I was a fool."

Arielle grumbled. "Dad was a jerk. Tommy was too. The thing is, it sounds to me like Tommy realized it, apologized for it, and has regretted it for years. Dad, on the other hand, was arrogant enough to think he could do anything he wanted. And he did, until it caused his death. He apologized in the letter, but he also confessed he wasn't going to change his ways. It's good he's finally out of your life."

"Don't speak that way of him."

"Stop defending him Mom. He cheated on you, he cheated his family, he tried to cheat life and it got him. Much as I loved him, I have to agree with Arielle, our father was a jerk, and he got what he deserved. You have to stop blaming yourself for his stupid choices. You should have left him. You thought you were doing what was best for us. We get that. Isn't it about time you do what's best for you?"

Kendra opened her mouth to speak, but Arielle placed her palm over her mouth.

"She's right. Adults make choices. Tommy made them. You made them. Dad made them. Now you get to make more. But this time, you are free to do what your heart truly desires. No mother telling you what you should do. No husband controlling you, while cheating on you. No young daughters at home for you to take care of, largely alone.

"Tomorrow really is the first day of new life for each of us. It will be much easier for us to leave if we know you will open your mind and your heart to whatever God offers next. Something tells me He doesn't want you to stay so shattered."

Kendra buried her face in Arthur's soft fur. They were right but she wasn't sure how to figure out what "next" was.

"Could you two clean up the hot chocolate mess I made? I think I will take a walk."

"Sure thing."

Arielle went inside as Adrienne lingered. "Um, Mom?"

"Yes?"

"There's something you should know. Yesterday we mailed a card to Tommy. It had sand dollars and starfish on the outside and inside we wrote, 'MMM.'"

CHAPTER SEVENTEEN

ENDINGS

The Turtle Shack
Labor Day, Present

endra kissed her finger and touched it to the faded photo on the shelf by the closet. It had warmed her heart to see the photo still in a place of prominence when she opened for the nesting season. It was her father the day Mimosa Beach Commissioners dedicated the Arthur J. Thomas Turtle Foundation and opened the shack the first time. Even in the years since his death, the photo remained on the shelf.

"Arthur, sit and stay." The puppy had been pulling tools and buckets out of the corner as fast as she put them away. At this rate, she'd never get the building closed for the year.

She removed all of the summer's record sheets from the clipboards and placed them in the folder she'd send to the foundation and the conservatory. She'd already boarded up the outside and sealed the windows. The last time she and Pa had closed for the season together was the summer before he died. Stan had been furious at her for taking the girls to the beach for Labor Day weekend instead of going to the chalet with his family. Many times in the past few years, she's been thankful for what was their last beach weekend with him, even though they didn't know it at the time.

The Turtle Shack
Labor Day 2011

Pa locked the door, then jiggled the padlock a few times to be sure it was secure. He brushed his hands and smiled at me.

"Well, Skeezix, another summer ends."

I grinned. "You haven't called me that for a long time."

"I know. Just seemed right. What time is Stan expecting you back?"

I drew toe-doodles in the sand. "I doubt he's given it any thought or care. But the girls need to get back tonight so we can back-to-school shop tomorrow."

"Then how about we take us a walk before going back?"

"I'd like that."

He looped my hand through the crook of his arm and headed to the surf. We walked along at the apex of the waves rolling in with the tide. The water was warm from the summer, and the sand squished between my toes. Beach walks with him had always been one of my favorite things.

He bent down and kissed the top of my head.

"You and me, we belong here at the sea. No matter how hard we try to live on the land, the sand and ocean are in us. Don't stay away so long. Okay?"

"I'll do better."

Pa stared out over the ocean and puffed on his pipe.

"Don't think I'll ever understand the ways of love."

"Love? What's that got to do with Stan?"

"Aw, honey, you know the man loves you…as best he can. It's your decision what you do next."

"I know. You waited for Mother."

He placed his fingers over my lips. "Different situation. Different time. But whatever you choose to do, do it with confidence and strength. And prayer."

I nodded.

We walked around the inlet and watched the rough waters where the ocean meets the sound. Then we looked over at the water park Tommy was just beginning. Pa wrapped his arm around my shoulder.

"There's no explaining why things went the way they did. Tommy messed up. You chose Stan. Both of you made some rash life choices. I know where both of your hearts live and always will. Kendra, you must be patient, faithful to God, your husband, your girls and yourself. True love wins. Look at my life. I'm living proof that it does."

"I hope you're right, Pa."

"I am. Now, let's go get you and my girls packed up. We'll have many more times here."

🐢

The Turtle Shack
Present

"But we didn't have more times here, Pa. Other than Thanksgiving, Christmas break, and the few days of summer before you died —that was it for us."

Arthur whimpered. He had actually stayed in that sit command much longer than expected.

"That's a good boy. Okay, come here." He raced to her and kissed her toes. "You would have loved Pa. But now it's time to lock things up."

The puppy looked as if he understood every word she spoke. "Let's take a slow walk home. Like me, everyone wants one more day on the water before heading home for the season."

She closed the padlock and jiggled it like Pa used to do. "Old habits die hard."

Shouldering her backpack, she turned toward the bay. After today, island life would slow down.

She walked along the water's edge, stopping to pick up and study shells and rocks. Snow white or pink rocks and unbroken shells deemed worthy of her shell jar got shoved into her pockets. Arthur chased sand crabs and shooed the sand pipers away. He was the self-appointed guardian of the water's edge.

Kendra glanced across the sound at the water park. The low-tide flag had just been removed. Boats were docking. Laughter and screams of joy echoed across the bay. She threw a broken shell into the water, then sat down and hugged her knees to her chin. The ripples from the boat in the center of Bay Lake made it to the shore and tickled her toes. Arthur sat at her feet and looked out over the water with her. She swore the dog knew her thoughts sometimes.

She scratched his ears before resuming the walk. "I guess a part of me expected there really was a plan B—or at least a plan next."

Three weeks had passed since the girls told her about the card. Obviously, her anger at them for sending the card was unfounded. Despite her doubt, she'd sat under that danged tree every afternoon the first week. Nothing happened. So much for the power of MMM.

Kendra stopped at the end of the island and sat on some old pilings. Arthur chased sand crabs. The weeks since they closed the turtle box and the girls moved out had been quiet. But she enjoyed the peaceful beach with most of the tourists gone.

Kendra picked up a few shell pieces and pitched them into the breakers. She looked up to the sky. "It's time to be honest with myself, isn't it, God? I can't pin all of the blame on everyone else. I choose right here, right now to end this codependence, justification, and pouting."

Yes, Tommy had been unfaithful. But she'd been eighteen and could have refused to go to Europe. Maybe she'd been unfaithful first—unfaithful to their plans. And Stan. The man married her knowing her heart belonged to someone else. And she knew his reputation as a player. Still, they married. No one made them. And she chose to stay with him.

High tide was sweeping into the sound like an angry monster. It reminded her of the anger she'd allowed to sweep into her heart over the years and take away her joy. She drew doodles in the sand with her toes.

"Arthur, I can't blame anyone else. I made my own decisions. I never thought I deserved a happy ending. But I did. I do."

She turned away from the water.

"Come on, puppy. It's time to figure out what my happy ending will look like when TJ's trial ends. Let's start at the coffee shop. And, maybe after we get home, I'll just chop that old mimosa tree down."

CHAPTER EIGHTEEN

BEGINNINGS

*A*t the ferry access road, Kendra removed Arthur's leash from her backpack and attached it to his collar. He crouched. "Oh, stop the pitiful puppy thing. You're not being punished. You've got to wear a leash in town. It'll be worth your frustration. I'll get a bag of those puppy treats for you as I sip my super decadent large extra whip caramel latte."

His ears perked at the word treat, and he started doing his happy prance.

They walked the five blocks to the café. Kendra placed her order, then sat down at a table overlooking the water. She picked Arthur up and sat him in the chair beside her.

"Okay, what shall we do first after I chop the tree down?"

His tail thumped as he crunched another treat.

"I have to make a list of projects for Master Renovators and let them schedule things in the most efficient order. Getting rid of the tree and maybe putting a gazebo in its place will be first order of business. We'll be able to enjoy it until it gets too cold. "

Arthur barked agreement.

Who'd have thought by summer's end she'd be ready to get rid of the tree? She should have turned loose of the past long ago.

She clapped her hands then nodded.

"It's time, once and for all, to leave the memories in the turtle box, let the past end, and start a brand new chapter. Arthur, we'll be okay, just you and me."

She finished her latte. "Let's go home, buddy."

By the time they arrived home, her resolve to jettison the past gave her a new focus. She stopped at the mailbox and studied her house. The new paint would be sky blue with darker trim. The porch would wrap around the entire house. The sun-room off the kitchen would become an all-season room. How she'd love sitting there in the winter, enjoying a fire in the stove, and watching the sound.

Kendra inhaled the crisp air blowing in from the water.

She opened the mailbox, hoping for another one of the silly cards the girls had sent her every few days. They shared their experiences as new homeowners and teachers. The stories she could write from her daughters' escapades. Before she closed the box something drew her attention. She reached inside and pulled out a single mimosa flower. How in the world?

She eyed the trees lining the street. Not one still in bloom. The flowers had been spent by the beginning of August. There was no way that flower had been there all of that time. Besides, it was pink and feathery. Fresh.

She pondered it as she walked to the back of the house.

"Come on, Arthur, I'll get the axe."

He raced around the house. She caught up to him as he stopped in the side yard and barked. He picked something up and ran back to her.

"What'cha got?"

He slinked toward her like he was in trouble and dropped another mimosa flower at her feet. Kendra frowned. "What?"

She placed it in her hand with the other one and stared at her tree. No more blossoms there either. But dotting her yard, the sidewalk around the house, the porch, the door jamb, and the porch swing were what had to be hundreds of pink mimosa flowers.

Kendra sat down on the bottom step and stared at them. It looked like a random storm dropped pink flowers on her property alone.

Arthur ran from one flower to the next. Some he sniffed then sneezed when they tickled his nose. Others he'd pick up and toss away. Every now and then, he'd grab one and run under the porch with it.

As she pondered them, she began to see a pattern. The flowers made a circular path through her yard, ending under the tree. They actually looked like a pillow. Only one man she knew of would cover her yard with pink snow.

She ran around the yard alternately flicking the petals with her toes, then picking handfuls up and tossing them into the air. Arthur chased after her.

At the tree she sat down in the center of the flower pillow. She lay back and closed her eyes. Arthur stretched down alongside her, resting his head on her shoulder.

Then he barked.

Kendra opened her eyes and looked up into the chocolate-brown eyes she'd loved forever.

"Hey."

Her heart pounded the Tommy rhythm. He was stretched across the lower limb, the same one he used to make fun of her from. She smiled.

He jumped out of the tree. "Thought you'd never get home."

"How long did you plan to wait?"

"As long as it took."

Tommy sat beside her and brushed a stray curl out of her face. "I've been away for a few weeks. I'm opening a water park in Maryland next summer. Getting permits and construction plans was a bigger endeavor than expected. When I got home, I found the note your daughters sent."

"I about disowned them for that. Then you didn't come, so I decided it didn't matter. They led me to believe you'd think I wrote it. How'd you know?"

A blush spread over his cheeks. She hadn't seen a Tommy blush for years.

"I know your handwriting, Kenna—how you word things. And I knew it wasn't you. The girls had told me you were sharing the turtle box memories with them, so I put two and two together. I'm sorry I wasn't in town."

She pointed to the yard. "The flowers. How?"

He winked. "An old man I held in high regard used to freeze them fresh and give them to a pretty lady. I've been freezing them for years, hoping I might have a pretty lady to give them to one day. Figured you fit the bill."

Tommy took one of the flowers and placed it in her hair. Then caught the tear tracking down her face on his finger and kissed it.

"I found something."

He reached in his shirt pocket and pulled out a perfect sand dollar. "Arielle and Adrienne told me your other one broke. God washed this on the beach today just for you."

Kendra opened her mouth, but nothing came out. She turned the sand dollar over in her hands and held it to her chest. Was this really happening?

"I know. I feel it too. I have something else. They've been in my safe for years. After I spread the flowers in the yard, I went to the bank and got them."

He took a little black box out of his jeans pocket. "A long time ago, I told you we'd have real ones someday."

Kendra's breath caught.

Tommy knelt in front of her. "I don't want to rush things, Kenna. I know we have a lot to work through. But could you work with me on the happily-ever-after thing?"

He opened the box. Nestled inside were two matching rings. Gold bands one with one a diamond and the other a smoke topaz.

Again, no words. She nodded and held her hand toward his. He placed one ring on her finger then slid the larger one on his.

He pulled her into his lap and, under the mimosa, kissed her the way he used to. Maybe she wouldn't chop the old tree down after all.

The Beginning

AUTHOR'S NOTE

I love creating new locations based upon my favorite places. I remember spending many summer vacations at Jekyll Island, GA. I also had family members with cottages at Topsail and Nags Head, North Carolina. I have spent many memorable weeks at Topsail and day trips at Nag's Head. Mimosa Beach comes from my fond memories of Jekyll Island and Topsail. While it's a location created in my imagination, anyone who has ever spent time on the Barrier Islands might see similarities.

If you're ever in the Surf City, North Carolina area, I highly recommend a visit to the Karen Beasley Sea Turtle Rescue and Rehabilitation Center. The amazing staff and volunteers from this facility inspired my character, Kendra's, involvement in sea turtle tracking, recording, and rescue.

Turtle Box Memories is Chandra Lynn Smith's second novel. Her first, *The Light Holding Her,* is a novella in *Coming Home, a Tiny House Collection.* Chandra, a 2015 Genesis winner, writes contemporary fiction filled with inspiration, intrigue, romance, and dogs. Thirty years as a Certified Professional Dog Trainer provides her with a variety of canine characters. Chandra and her husband are the proud parents of four sons and joyous grandparents to the most beautiful granddaughter in the world. They live on a small farm in South Central Pennsylvania. Their house is often filled with their two dogs, all four sons, two fiancés, one granddaughter, any number of friends, and anywhere from four to eight "grand-dogs."

You can find her at www.ChandraLynnSmith.blogspot.com or www.ChandraLynnSmith.com.

If you enjoyed reading Kendra and Tommy's story, please go to Amazon.com and post a review!

~~Be sure to watch for Adrienne and Arielle's stories in book 2 of the Healing Sands Series coming in 2019~~

Also look for Chandra's first novella. *The Light Holding Her* is in the collection of novels about characters living in Tiny Houses. *Coming Home, a Tiny House Collection* is available on Amazon.